Splintered Reflections

By
Laura Kelly

ISBN: 978-1-62747-001-8
eISBN: 978-1-62747-003-2

Book cover designed by Sasha Scully
www.sashascully.com

Since becoming an author has been a dream of mine for as long as I can remember, I would like to dedicate this book to anyone who has a dream – Never Give Up on Your Dream.

Chapter One

The steamy mist parted as I made my way to the mirror. The question was vibrating in my mind as I moved closer and closer to the mirror, causing emotions to stir – a mixture of dread and anticipation churning inside my stomach just like the haze that was swirling around me. I could smell the sweet scent of citrus floating in the air as I saw my form appear in the mirror. I was a stranger looking back at me. I took a deep breath, letting the refreshing scent fill my lungs, and hoping that the scent would wash away my darkness. I swallowed before slowly letting my breath out and asking the question – Who am I?

The steam from the shower surrounded me, touching my skin like a forgotten kiss. I continued to stare into the dark pupils that were glaring back at me, my long brown hair hanging in damp strands around my oval face. I moved closer to the mirror, hoping that if I stared long enough I would see that the answer had always been there. I just needed to look a little deeper, a little harder. I took another deep breath before asking the question again.

"Who am I?" This time, desperation was in my voice. Blank, almost lifeless eyes continued to look back at me. I had to wonder if they were mocking me. I looked deeper into the eyes, patiently waiting for the answer to explode like a series of fireworks. Yet every morning it was the same – silence.

The only sound was my breathing, steady at first, but soon increasing with the hope that today might be the day. Who was that person staring back at me? The question was always swirling in my mind, sometimes making me dizzy; most of the time, the question was just an endless hum.

A pit of disappointment in the center of my heart expanded. Why do I continue with this sad ritual, I thought? I pushed myself away from the mirror with a heavy sigh, thinking that maybe tomorrow I would get an answer. I dragged myself back to the bedroom, my shoulders slumped and my heart heavy. I slid my body back into the security of my bed, pulling the covers over my head to block out the morning light that was trying to break through to my room and let me know that it was the start of a new day. Maybe if I sank deeper into my covers I could escape the loneliness and guilt that surrounded me. The one person who could give me some glimmer of an answer to my question was gone. I cried myself back to sleep, knowing that she would never return.

Chapter Two

The backstage of the auditorium was filled with muttering, or "la, la, la," as everyone was whispering or warming up their voice in some way. I was standing alone, my eyes closed, humming my solo – Silent Night – to myself. Even though I had practiced and practiced, almost to the point of losing my voice, butterflies were still fluttering in my stomach and my knees were shaking. Miss O'Brien clapped her hands, letting us know it was time to take our spot on the tiered risers. Somehow, I was able to float my shaky legs to my spot. I was standing in the front, next to Bobby, who also had a solo. I glanced at Bobby to see that he had his eyes closed, and his lips were moving. I smiled, glad to know that I was not the only one who was nervous.

The dark-red curtains parted with a soft swoosh – and there they were, staring at us – the faces of our mothers and fathers. I swallowed down the fear. All those eyes were looking at me, I thought. A hush reverberated through the large room, and then there was silence. The only sound I could hear was the beating of my heart and the shaking of my knees. I prayed that Bobby or Miss O'Brien could not hear the thump, thump of my heart that was echoing in my ears. I closed my eyes, willing myself to be calm. "I can do this," I said to myself. Miss O'Brien tapped her skinny wand on the music stand that was separating her from us. The tap, tap, tap of the wand was the command for us to stand taller and to take a breath. Miss O'Brien nodded to Mrs. Davis, who softly touched the first keys on the piano. The skinny wand drifted in my direction, letting me know it was time to start. I took a deep breath, letting the words I knew so well float from me to the crowd. The scent of pine was wafting through the room, and so was my voice. The crowd was smiling, and gently bobbing their heads from side to side. And there was Mom, sitting alone in the back of the auditorium. I tilted my head to see that Mom, too, was smiling. My heart was bursting with happiness. The choir joined in, singing the chorus. The fluttering in my body was soon replaced with a humming that gradually increased. Even after the song had ended, the humming continued, causing a slight vibration in my body. The crowd stood, clapping and cheering in admiration. A happiness I had never felt before coursed through me. I was floating like an angel.

The Christmas performance ended and the singing was replaced with chattering, as kids and their parents loitered around the large auditorium. I craned my head around and through the crowd, trying to find Mom. I should have known she would be in the back, waiting for me. I pushed my tiny body through the sea of legs until I could see Mom standing with no one around her. I ran towards her, my white robe billowing like a cloud. She bent down with her arms opened wide. I jumped into her arms, wrapping my tiny arms around her neck. She hugged me closer to her and swung me in a slow circle. Our checks touched, and the scent of roses flooded my nose.

I stirred, forcing myself back out of bed and into my harsh reality. Mom was no longer around to swing me in a circle. I let out a heavy sigh, pushing my one happy memory that had happened so many, many years ago into the depths of my mind, pulling it out whenever I needed to escape from my own private nightmare.

It was always just Mom and me. There was never a dad. I never knew if he was alive or dead, since Mom never mentioned him. And so I thought the worst – that he was dead. He had to have been, based on Mom's reaction when I finally gathered the courage to ask her. Typically, when spouses lose their significant others, there would be silence, with a longing in their eyes, whenever the lost spouse's name is mentioned. Not with Mom. She would say, with a sharp tone in her voice, that he was gone. I could hear the door to her heart slap shut, letting me know that Dad was not a topic she wanted to discuss. I shivered from the abrupt tone that escaped her lips. He must have hurt her deeply. After that, I never asked Mom about Dad, even though I longed to know if she loved him. They had to have loved each other at one time, since they had me, and so I clung to that one glimmer of hope.

Hoping and daydreaming were my companions, since Mom was rarely around. Mom was always working. And when she was home, she was exhausted from work. Since I was afraid of bothering Mom, I spent most of my time daydreaming.

Like most little girls, I dreamt about being a princess. However, in my dream, the queen and king had died in a horrible hunting accident, leaving me alone to rule the kingdom until my Prince Charming climbed the castle wall to be with me. This daydream was always followed by a heavy sigh, since I am not a princess, and my mom and dad were not a queen or a king. Since I was just a little girl trying to survive my gloomy world of confusion and despair, I pushed that fantasy down, just as deep as my single happy childhood memory.

I tried to stay positive for Mom, but it never seemed to help. She would just sit at the table after a long day of working, pushing her food around and looking off into the distance as if searching for something or maybe someone. Silence engulfed the room – with an occasional scraping of the fork against the plate, followed by a heavy sigh. I would beat myself up trying to think of something, anything to say, but instead of finding the right words I would end up feeling either afraid or defeated. I was just a shadowy figure sitting across from her.

My one true happy place was my bedroom. My room was the place where I could play music. It was the place where I could sing, dance, and escape. It was the place where I would dream. I would dream of being popular at school. I would dream of my father walking into our home after being lost in the jungle during one of his many dangerous expeditions. I would dream about my guardian angel whisking me away from my unhappiness.

There were times when I truly believed that Mom was either jealous of my bedroom or that she had snapped. She would run into my room and start ripping the posters from the wall, and shoving books from the bookshelf onto the floor. She yanked the comforter, with my neatly organized stuffed animals, off the bed. The animals flew into the air and landed, scattered, on the floor. While she was tearing my room apart, she would be yelling at me. Even today, I still hear the hateful words that would spew from her lips: "I wish you had never been born," and "You ruined my life." Each hateful word sliced into every fiber of my being – as I crouched in the corner, covering my head with my arms – crying and wishing that her rampage would soon end.

She eventually stopped once the walls were bare; once she was breathless and too tired to tear one more poster or throw one more book. My room looked like a battlefield, with the floor covered with torn posters, stuffed animals, books, and clothes. I felt like a casualty of a war that I didn't know existed. Mom never apologized. Mom would never cry. She would slowly make her way through the mess she'd created – leaving me alone, huddling and crying, in the corner. I was left to piece my room back together. I was left frightened, confused, and damaged. I was left alone, begging my guardian angel to take me away.

Each time she went through her emotional storm, my happy place got a little sadder, and dreaming got a lot harder.

And then one day, I was the one who snapped. I don't know if it was her tearing my newest poster into shreds, or if I had just had enough. I yelled back, telling her that I wished she would go away and never come back. And for once, my guardian angel listened. The next day, Mom and I left the house the way we did every morning. I went to school. Mom went to work. I came back to an empty and dark house, waiting at the table for Mom to come home. That was a week before my high school graduation.

There was no reason to crane my neck the way I had when I was five, looking for Mom in the crowd, when I was waiting to receive my high school diploma. There was no reason to push my way through the crowd after the graduation ceremony to find Mom standing in the back, because Mom was not there. You see, Mom never came home that day.

Chapter Three

The air in the bathroom was heavy, not because of the steam from my hot shower, but from the darkness that was swallowing me. Even the brightness still lingering from my citrus soap was not easing the gloom. I pulled the thick cotton robe closer around me, hoping to keep the warmth from the hot shower in. I stood looking at my reflection in the mirror – the dull, hazel eyes; the thin, brown strands hanging lifeless around my face; the thin, pink lips that rarely formed a smile; and yes, the shroud of darkness I continued to carry.

It was another day of looking into the mirror and asking the question. I knew it would be another day of silence. Would my life stop if I did not ask the question? What was the definition of insanity – doing the same thing over and over again and expecting different results? Perhaps I *am* insane.

I opened the medicine cabinet and admired the various bottles that were neatly organized on the two shelves. I took a clear, intricate glass bottle out of the cabinet. I examined the bottle, admiring how the bathroom light reflected off the glass before pushing the top of the bottle and filling the air with a spray of roses. I took a deep breath, letting the scent permeate my senses and awaken the memory. My eyes swelled with the pain of that memory. I blinked back the tears, quickly placing the bottle back onto the shelf and grabbing one of the many brown bottles that I had collected over the past year. I shook the bottle, making a rhythmic rattling of the pills against their plastic container. I thought of a song that I hadn't heard in a while. I thought about singing. I opened the bottle and thought of Mom. The guilt came flooding back, pounding itself onto my body. I stumbled back, dropping the bottle to the floor. The tiny white pills bounced up and down several times, making a soft tick, tick, tick sound until they finally settled, scattered against the floor. A wave of dizziness washed over me, causing me to slump to the bathroom floor, my back propped across the wall. The coldness from the tile was creeping through my robe and into my bones. I hugged my legs closer to me, hoping to bring back some warmth, but I knew it was too late. I shoved what pills I could find back into the bottle and crawled back to bed, where I knew I would be warm. Where I knew I could let the world pass by me and my sorry life.

I pulled the thick blue comforter over my body, hoping to regain some warmth, but it was too late. The cold fingers of dread were already seeping into my soul. I wrapped the comforter tighter around my body, but it was useless. An uncontrollable shiver took over my body. I took a deep breath, hoping it would wash away the dread and calm my nerves, but it did not work this time. Why do I keep doing this to myself, I thought? I knew I needed to stop mentally beating myself up with my sad memories, and that pathetic question. The Doc was right – I needed to step beyond the security blanket that I'd created, and start living. But it's so hard. Oh, Mom, I miss you.

Chapter Four

It was a short drive to the campus, leaving me little time to think of all the excuses of why I should turn back and all the reasons why I should continue forward. Instead, I thought about my first day of high school and how terrified I was. I wanted to slap my hand against my forehead for allowing the past to return. But the one thing I've learned was that my past was deeply ingrained into every fiber of my body.

I remember the stories of how seniors would do awful things to freshmen on the first day of school – stories such as the seniors locking the freshmen in their lockers, or a freshman having to carry a senior's backpack or books. Perhaps they were only stories, since nothing bad had ever happened to me and I never saw anything bad happen to another student. Even so, I'd always been nervous whenever I walked down the hallway to my locker. I was constantly looking over my shoulder, especially if I heard anyone close to me. I was terrified to go to the cafeteria for lunch, and never did. I was afraid all eyes would be on me the minute I walked into the cafeteria. I would imagine them whispering "Freak," or "Boring Cathy" as I walked by their table, tray in hand, trying not to fall. I stayed away from the cafeteria, waiting to eat when I got home, my stomach constantly growling throughout the afternoon. Other times I would quickly eat a small sandwich at my locker before going to the library to study. The teachers were nice to me, but sometimes I believe that they too thought I was just a shadow in the classroom. I was never a memorable student.

I lurched my beat-up green Honda Civic to a stop in the huge parking lot of the college campus. I looked beyond the cracked gray dashboard to see a set of stairs, leading up to a sea of cement. Red-brick buildings surrounded the cement, with an occasional tree sprinkling green among the brick red. I wrapped my fingers around the steering wheel, willing myself to let go – willing myself to leave my car.

I opened the driver's door and a cool breeze rushed into the stuffy car. The breeze felt soothing against my cheeks, but did little for the emotions that were churning. I pushed myself out of the car and looked up at the wisps of clouds that were slowly drifting across the blue sky. It was mid-August, but it seemed as though fall wanted to arrive before its time. The green leaves in the trees that lined the staircase were rustling. I had to wonder if the trees despised change as much as I did, and that the rustling was their way of protesting. "Stop being a chicken, Cathy," I softly said out loud, knowing that no one was around to hear me.

I walked up the small flight of stairs and across the campus to a group of brick buildings. My hands were cold and clammy, even though the sun was shining. I flexed my fingers, hoping to bring some warmth to them. "I can do this, I can do this," I repeated to myself, with each affirmation matched by a step. My legs were getting heavier with each step as I questioned where my legs were taking me and why. Each step was harder and harder to make. It felt as though the plaza had turned into mud, and I was stuck. Maybe the plaza knew what I suspected – that this was a waste of time. Whatever was I thinking, starting college at my age? I know I am smart, but am I smart enough to be in college? I could just stay hiding under my comforter and not go to school. Would that be so bad, I thought?

"What if" began to swirl around in my mind like little snowflakes. What if I don't finish this walk across campus? What if I stay in my apartment and my warm bed? What if I turn around and go home?

I quietly whispered "what if" several times as I scanned the campus. There were a few students walking across the campus, but they were too far away to hear my personal debate. I did imagine one of them answering my question, and it was not favorable – their thoughts humming to me and saying, "Why is boring Cathy here?" followed by "She does not deserve to be here."

I abruptly stopped and stared at a row of brick buildings that was just a few feet ahead, the fear and self-doubt bubbling back up. I turned to walk away from the brick buildings and back to my car when the breeze returned, brushing itself lightly against my cheek. I looked up to see that the wisps of clouds had transformed into white, puffy ones. Calmness washed over my body as I gazed into the sky, knowing that my guardian angel was smiling down at me. The breeze was her way of letting me know that I was safe.

I took a deep breath, letting it out slowly. I moved my gaze back to the row of brick buildings and placed one foot in front of the other, continuing my march and resuming my mental affirmation, "I can do this, I can do this." I took another glance from one side of the campus to the other to see if anyone was watching me or listening to me. There was no one in sight.

My heart felt a little lighter and my determination a little stronger by the time I reached my destination. I scanned the row of buildings, looking for the registration office. I turned to the right and walked a few more steps before standing in front of a smoky glass door. "Registration Office" was painted in large white letters across the door. The bold letters were calling out to me, almost daring me to enter. I swallowed down my fear and grabbed the handle to open the door. I entered a small lobby area with a long orange couch across from the entrance and several matching chairs. There was a long counter behind the couch. I went up to the counter and saw a young woman with very short, light-brown hair, sitting at a desk to the right of the counter. She seemed to be absorbed in the latest update on Facebook, since several minutes passed by without her noticing me.

I cleared my throat before saying "excuse me." The girl yelped and jumped, then turned her head slightly in my direction.

"Oh, I didn't hear you," she said, in an extremely high-pitched voice.

I winced, hoping that she hadn't noticed my reaction. Her voice reminded me of grade school, when the teacher would write on the chalkboard, and occasionally the chalk would make a screeching sound across the board that would send shivers up and down the spine of every child in the classroom. I didn't think anyone's voice could reach that high. I had to wonder if that was her real voice, or maybe I'd really scared her.

I shook the thought out of my head.

"Can I help you?" she said with a slight shriek, moving her attention from the computer screen to me. I guess that really was her real voice, I thought.

"Hmmm, yes, I would like to register for classes." I said, being mindful of my own voice.

"Okay," she squeaked, jumping out of her chair and moving to the counter. She was definitely excited to help me. "Do you know which classes you would like to take?"

I felt like she just asked me something in a foreign language. My face must have expressed what I was thinking, since she tilted her head and examined me.

"Are you okay?" she asked, again with the high-pitched voice.

Classes. I'd never really thought about what classes I should take. The fear and the rumbling in my stomach returned. I was back in high school, and I wasn't able to answer the question that the teacher had just asked. I'm certain my forehead was dripping with sweat, because I was getting very warm.

"Hmmm, I guess I don't know," I said, in a very low voice, moving my eyes down to the counter. I was nervous and embarrassed.

"That's not a problem," she shrilled. Obviously my flinching did not have an effect on her, since her voice seemed to get higher and higher each time she spoke. How was that possible, I thought.

"I think you should start by looking at the class catalog," she said, pulling a very thick catalog from underneath the counter. There was a soft thud when she placed the catalog on the counter. I mindlessly flipped through the pages, staring at the endless gray of the words on the white background.

I had no idea what I wanted to take, or what I should take. Typically, when someone goes to college, they have a general idea of what they want to study. I remember kids in high school saying they were going to be a doctor, or a lawyer, or a teacher. I never really thought about what I wanted to be when I grew up. I took the classes my counselor in high school said I should take, never questioning or thinking. I just followed. I needed someone to tell me what to do. I blew out a heavy sigh, wishing Mom were here. Maybe she could tell me what classes I should take.

I stopped flipping through the pages and looked from the catalog to the girl.

"I really don't know what I should take," I whispered, half hoping that she would not hear me. The other half of me was feeling ashamed.

Now it was my turn to be speaking a foreign language, since her eyes got as big as the golden hoops dangling from her ears.

"Okay," she said very slowly, as if she didn't know what else to say – or maybe she thought if she spoke the words slowly, I would understand her.

"Why don't you sit over in the lobby and take your time looking through the catalog. Maybe something will jump out at you," she said, adding a little squeal when pronouncing the word "you."

I looked down at the catalog and rolled my eyes. This girl was not a lot of help, I thought.

"Is there anyone I could talk to or who could help me?" I pleaded.

She blew out a heavy sigh before telling me that there were counselors, but that they were not working today.

Great, I thought to myself. I reluctantly lifted the thick catalog off the counter and walked out the smoky glass door. I had to sit down, and I wasn't going to sit in the lobby and risk having "high-pitch girl" stare at me. I needed to feel the breeze that had greeted me earlier. I didn't know if the ringing in my head was from the girl's high-pitched voice or the anxiety of not knowing what to do. There was still time to walk back to my car and drive back to my little apartment. "I'm such a failure," I thought.

I thought of another "what if." What if I really don't know what I wanted to study or be when I grew up? What am I going to do? Why was it easier for others and not for me? Again, a flood of questions assaulted me. Maybe it goes back to not knowing who I am.

I found a comfortable-looking bench underneath three small trees. The trees provided some shade. I sat down on the bench with a thud. It felt good to sit down. I looked down at the catalog, its weight heavy on my lap. I don't know which was heavier, the catalog or not knowing which classes to take. My shoulders drooped as I turned one page after another, this time taking a closer look at my possibilities.

"It can't be that hard to pick a class," I muttered to myself. Maybe I should randomly pick a page.

I closed my eyes, hoping my fingers would land on something exciting. But what I got was French and anatomy. Not good, I thought. I'd tried French for two semesters in high school and hated it. The only thing I remember was counting to ten and saying hello and goodbye. The anatomy class had prerequisites. Obviously, this method was not working. I had to wonder where my guardian angel was right now. Shouldn't she be sending me some type of sign to guide me?

I tossed the catalog to the side and tilted my head back in frustration. The sun was filtering through the leaves, its warmth inviting on my skin. The ringing in my ears had been replaced by a soft, pulsating hum. I let out a long and heavy sigh, releasing the anxiety that had been trapped inside me. Looking at the sky was calming. I gazed at the blue sky, watching the white, puffy clouds slowly dancing across the sky. I was mesmerized by the way the clouds changed shape, wondering why clouds move the way they do. I remembered lying on the cool, green grass as a child, watching the clouds and letting my worries be swept away.

And with a single blink of my eyes it happened – the answer broke through. I pulled my head up from my daze and back to the catalog. My fingers quickly flipped through the pages to the classes they were being drawn to. I earmarked the pages my fingers flew to – biology, psychology, and creative writing. Probably not the most logical grouping of classes, but it was a good start. I included a business class to add some practicality to my haphazard choices.

I floated like one of the puffy white clouds that hovered above me to the registration building. "I'm going to be a college student," I mentally sang to myself; the soft humming in the back of my mind providing the melody for my song.

Chapter Five

The fog was swirling around my feet as I slowly moved towards a glimmer of light that was breaking through the darkness. Fear was churning in my stomach. I knew I was late for something important, but I wasn't sure what it was. Dark figures with white eyes were watching me. The dark figures were surrounding me, a crowd of darkness drifting closer and closer around me, trapping me, suffocating me. When I moved forward, so did the dark figures. I looked down, hoping to avoid their glaring eyes. But that did not help. I could still feel the heat from their stares. I inched closer and closer to the sliver of light to see that the light was coming from a door. I was getting anxious, thinking that the door could be my escape from the stares that were burning into my flesh. The dark figures were whispering, but I could not understand what they were saying. Soon the whispers turned to laughter. I covered my ears and shouted, "Why are you laughing at me?" I walked faster and faster, my feet breaking through the fog, hoping that I could flee from the evil voices and piercing white eyes. But I could not. I was surrounded. Panic was bubbling inside me. I frantically turned to one side and then the other to see that the light had disappeared. Then with a simple blink, the fog and the swarm of dark figures parted, bringing the door into view. I reached for the handle of the door and saw my reflection in the window. I was naked.

My eyes opened and I bolted upright in my bed, wrapping my arms around myself checking to see if I was naked. I let out a sigh, feeling the softness of my cotton t-shirt. It was just a dream, I thought, taking in several gulps of air and trying to get my breathing under control. It was just a dream, I said, falling back onto my bed and pulling my blue comforter around me. It was just a dream, I thought, looking at the ceiling and blinking the sleep out of my eyes.

I stayed in bed for what seemed like an hour, willing myself to leave the warmth and security of the comforter that surrounded me. "You can do this, Cathy," I said out loud. I slowly pulled the blue cover off my body and to the side, swinging my legs off the bed. I sat on the bed, wiggling my toes and convincing myself that it would be okay – just walk into the bathroom the way you do every morning.

I pushed myself off my bed and shuffled to the bathroom. The floor was cold, but my bare feet welcomed the coolness. I went to the mirror, afraid to see a naked reflection glaring back at me. I let out a sigh of relief when I saw my pink T-shirt and flannel shorts. I steadied myself against the bathroom sink and looked deep into my eyes. The hint of dark circles was peeking below my puffy eyes. A moan escaped my mouth, knowing that I did not have time to take a hot shower.

"Who are you?" I whispered. I was expecting the reflection to say "streaker" or "stripper"; instead there was only silence as the hazel eyes stared back at me. I was not frustrated. I was tired and scared. I splashed cold water on my face. The icy water was refreshing – and just what I needed to snap me back to reality.

I swallowed down the butterflies of fear that were rumbling in my stomach. What a great way to start my first day as a college student, I thought. I quickly pulled a brush through my unruly bed hair, placing it in a loose pony tail. Wisps of brown strands fell from the hair tie and oddly framed my oval face perfectly. I looked at myself in the mirror several times before grabbing my backpack and car keys. "Yes, I am wearing clothes," I said, closing the door and leaving my tiny apartment.

I drove to the campus, mentally walking to the classes I had today. Since I didn't like surprises, I'd gone to the campus yesterday to locate all of my classes. I did not want to be late to any of them. I did not want to ask for directions. I definitely did not want to be laughed at. I wanted to have some control, no matter how small it might be. My legs were not as heavy as they had been the first time I walked across the plaza. In fact, I almost felt normal. It also helped that no one else was around. But then again, who would be walking around the campus on a Sunday?

The campus was a lot different today than it was yesterday. Instead of having the campus all to myself, I was one of many students either heading to their first class or just milling around in small crowds, talking about their summer and comparing notes on the classes they were taking. I took a deep breath and maneuvered my way through the sea of students, hoping not to bump into anyone. I knew I could walk to each of my classes with my eyes closed, but I didn't. Maybe I should have, since I could feel their stares and strange glances following me. Flashes of last night's dream darted into my mind. Why were they looking at me, I thought? I know I didn't have anything strange on my face, and I wasn't naked, since I'd looked at myself at least three times before leaving the apartment.

21

I finally made it to my first class – creative writing. I took a seat in the back, hoping that no one would see me, hoping that I would become the shadow that I'd mastered so well in high school. Soon other students, mostly well-dressed girls, entered the room. I was stunned when I saw how dressed up they were. They looked as though they were going out on a date rather than attending a college class. I looked down at my own clothes, wondering if I was underdressed. I'd always thought that jeans and a T-shirt were the standard clothes for college. My shoulders drooped from the weight of my uncertainty, with the self-doubt resuming its place in the pit of my stomach. Did I miss the memo about how to dress for this class? I went back to looking at the other students, who were scattered throughout the large classroom. Most of the students took a seat in the middle. A few guys sat in the back row, but not next to me. I did notice that the guys were wearing jeans, just like me, which eased my anxiety a bit. I found it interesting that the few students who decided to sit in the front row were all girls. I watched as they carefully removed their laptops from their big, fancy bags. They opened their laptops and sat upright, poised for class to begin.

Uncertainty rushed back into my mind, a tidal wave of self-doubt. Do I need a laptop, I thought? I was feeling unprepared, and I did not like it. Fear swept into the depths of my brain, and the butterflies morphed into bees, and then there was the hum. I sucked in a deep breath, hoping the air would calm my nerves.

"It will be okay, it will be okay," I whispered to myself, glad that no one was around to hear me. Maybe I could talk to the professor after class, to see if I need a laptop and to find out more about a dress code.

A gorgeous guy wearing khakis and a crisp white shirt with a blue tie strolled into the classroom, snapping me out of my mental discussion and back to the classroom. I had to take a second look at the man with the dark, wavy hair and wire-framed glasses, not because he was good looking but because he looked vaguely familiar. My mouth dropped when I saw him walk to the front of the class – as if he had done this numerous times before – as if he belonged there. I didn't think I was the only one whose mouth dropped, since the small talk that had been droning in the classroom came to an abrupt stop. He had everyone's attention. I had to wonder if he could feel their gaze. He didn't act like it; it was almost as though he had been through this routine before. He seemed so confident, with an aura of certainty radiating from him. I had to wonder what had captured my attention more: his confidence or his good looks.

I had to think that he was too good looking to be a professor, and definitely too young. Aren't most professors old and portly? I knew at that moment that I was not going to ask him anything after class. In fact, I wasn't certain if I would be able to concentrate in class at all. I forgot to ask myself, "What if the professor was gorgeous," when I was picking my classes. Would I still be sitting in the classroom if I knew the answer? Why did I sign up for this class, I thought? Oh yes – the clouds.

Silence hung heavy in the classroom. The entire class, captivated by his aura, watched as he walked to the board in the front of the room. He wrote his name – Mr. Hanson – followed by Creative Writing.

I looked around the room at the other students to see what they were doing. All of the students but one was hanging on every move that Professor Hanson made. The other girl was looking at me, or so it seemed. I quickly looked away after our eyes met. I'm certain I flushed. She was very pretty, with short golden hair that framed a porcelain face, with high cheekbones and a cute little nose. I'd always wanted high cheekbones, I thought.

She really did seem to fit the description of a modern Barbie, but not as plastic – maybe a bit more like Paris Hilton. I had to wonder if she had a small dog in her purse or backpack. She looked like she could definitely get away with it.

Maybe she was looking at someone else, I thought. I started to turn to see if that was true, when I remembered I was sitting in the back row. I nervously looked back at her, again wondering why she was looking at me when she could be looking at the cute professor. The pretty girl smiled, shrugged her shoulders, and turned her attention to the cute professor. She definitely exuded the same confidence as Professor Hanson.

Why would she smile at me? I am nobody, I thought. It was my turn to shrug and return my focus on Professor Hanson who was now writing a string of words on the board.

Professor Hanson placed the marker down and turned to face the classroom. His face seemed to be etched in stone. I had to wonder if he was human or some type of marble statue. And then he spoke. His voice was monotone, void of emotion. Words about what he hoped we would gain from his class during this semester floated out to the students as an Artic puff. He walked to a stack of paper sitting on his desk at the front of the room. All heads obediently followed him. I had to think the entire class was mesmerized by him, since the only sound was the soft crunching of Professor Hanson walking across the thin carpet. He picked up the stack and went from row to row, handing out a few sheets of paper to the person located at the start of each row. The smaller stack of paper made its way down the row, with each person taking one sheet from the stack.

My palms were getting clammy as Professor Hanson moved closer and closer to the back row, and to me. Yes, I was the first person in my row. He handed me the last of the paper without emotion. Our eyes locked as I took the paper. For a moment I felt trapped in his dark-brown eyes, magnified behind his glasses. I broke away to look down at my desk, and thanked him. My hands were shaking when I took a sheet of paper from the top and placed it on the desk next to my notebook. I had to get up from my seat to pass the rest to the next person since he was a few seats away from me. My legs were rubbery when I walked back to my desk.

Professor Hanson was discussing our first assignment as he strolled back to the front of the classroom and sat on the edge of his desk. The butterflies that had been rumbling in the pit of my stomach had been replaced with a hum that vibrated "Why am I here?" over and over. Fear was working its way back into my mind.

Professor Hanson said that our first assignment was an easy one that would give him an indication of our writing style and some information about us. He pushed himself up from the edge of his desk and moved to the board. He picked up the marker and wrote our assignment on the board, his stiff body gracefully moving with each word. My heart sank once he moved away from the board. Yes, I was in hell. The assignment was to write one or two sentences about ourselves.

I bowed my head to the blank piece of paper. Its whiteness was blinding me. I stared at it willing the words to appear, any words, because I did not know how to answer that question. I was wishing someone else would write something about me. I looked down my row. I could see a few students writing feverishly; some were staring off into space as if pondering the question. Soon they would return to their piece of paper to write whatever they were able to pull from their metal deliberation.

I returned my attention to the paper. It was still blank. I started to panic, feeling my body tremble. I glanced to my left, making sure no one was watching me, hoping that no one could see me shake. Maybe the shaking was all in my mind. I looked at my hand, hovering above the desk, to see that it was quivering. Yes, I am shaking, I thought. I closed my eyes, willing myself to stop shaking, willing myself to write something.

I opened my eyes and wrote my name on the upper right corner of the page, hoping that the act of writing my name would cause a breakthrough. It did not. At least the page was not as glaring. In fact, it looked more alive, with "Cathy Fitzpatrick" written in bold letters.

The sound of someone clearing their throat broke through my turmoil. There was someone behind me, their body casting a dull shadow onto the paper. Even though I could feel the heat of their gaze on the back of my neck, I felt chilled.

"Cathy, are you okay?" a cold voice whispered behind me.

I slowly cocked my head up to see the dark-brown eyes of Professor Hanson glaring down at me. I was hoping he could not see the tears that were starting to swell in my eyes. I was afraid to speak. I knew the dam that I was so desperately trying to hold back would break if I uttered a single word.

"You need to finish the assignment," he said in a low voice. I could feel the ice behind each word he spoke. The disappointment in his eyes added to emotions I was trying to force down.

I swallowed, trying to find my voice. My mind frantically searching for an answer – Who am I? Who am I? Right now I felt like a failure.

"I'm sorry, Professor Hanson. I cannot seem to find my pen. I know I had one in my bag but I must have lost it. I know that sounds like a crazy excuse." I stopped talking because one, he was looking at me with a raised eyebrow. And two, I was sounding like an idiot.

Professor Hanson took a pen from his pocket and handed it to me.

"You now have a pen." His voice was harsh, almost as though he was irritated by me.

I felt my face turn several shades of red, as I took the pen and whispered "Thank you." He did not say another word. Instead, he turned his back to me and walked down the aisle. I could feel every eye in the classroom on me now. "Oh, please let me just melt from my chair onto the floor," I silently cried. I wish I could transform into a shadow and float out of the classroom, never to return. I watched Professor Hanson return to the front of the classroom. I had to wonder if he could feel my gaze – if he could sense the frustration I was feeling.

I looked back at the piece of paper. It was still staring at me. The reason I signed up for this class drifted back into my mind, but this time like a strong gust of wind. My hand quickly scribbled across the paper – "Who I am is a constant question. What if I never get the answer to this question constantly haunts me."

I was certain my two cryptic lines would not satisfy the cold Professor Hanson. But that was how I felt, especially after looking into the darkness that were his eyes and feeling the eyes of everyone in the classroom. I am a failure.

I looked up to discover that I was the last person in the classroom. I was relieved to see that Professor Hanson wasn't looking at me as if waiting for me to finally finish the assignment. His attention was on the stack of papers, the answers that the other students had provided.

I slowly got up from my seat and grabbed the piece of paper, holding it as if it was my enemy. I stood as tall as I could and quietly walked towards Professor Hanson, focusing my attention on the top of his head. Perhaps if I tiptoed down the aisle, he would not hear me coming. I was lucky that he did not. I gently placed the piece of paper, words down, next to the pile. He looked up, tilting his head in my direction.

Dang, I said to myself. I really wish I could float right now. I knew I should have bolted out of the classroom once I placed the assignment on his desk.

Something of a smile crossed his tanned, chiseled face. He flipped the paper over to read what I had written. My heart sank when I saw the stony face reappear. This time I turned and rushed out of the classroom, crashing through the doors. I stood against the wall trying to catch my breath, willing myself to relax.

I wish I could say I had a good first day of class, but I cannot. I could still feel everyone staring at me, little pricks invading my skin. Were they the eyes of the cute professor or of the classroom? I pushed myself away from the wall and jogged across the campus to my next class, trying not to think of the last ten minutes. Instead, a mental debate of "Why am I here?" and "Yes I can do this!" assaulted my mind – with my self-doubt winning.

My next class was biology, and I had about five minutes before that class started. I slowed my pace, hoping that I would gain some type of composure. I reached the door of the Science building when I heard a tap, tap, tap behind me. I resumed my slow jog, afraid of the tap, tap, tap that was getting closer. My hand reached for the door when something touched my shoulder. I jumped, thinking Professor Hanson had decided that he did not like what I wrote and wanted me to redo the assignment, but that would be silly. Professor Hanson would not make a tap, tap sound as he walked. I turned to find a flushed "Paris Hilton" staring at me with her vivid blue eyes.

I stepped back, afraid that she was going to do something mean to me, remembering that this was the first day of school. Flashbacks of high school and lockers came rushing to my mind.

"Are you okay?" she asked. Her voice was sweet and soothing, definitely nothing like the high-pitched voice of the girl who helped me register for my classes.

Why would she be concerned for me, I thought?

I must have looked confused, since she repeated the question, this time her hand lightly touching my shoulder. I thought her hand would burn into my flesh. Instead, her soft touch and floral perfume sent a wave of comfort that flooded my senses. It reminded me of walking in a field of flowers with the sun beaming down on me. I looked down to see if she had a purse, and if that purse contained a small dog. I was disappointed when I did not see a cute little dog gawking at me. She did have a vibrant pink bag that was big enough to hold a little dog.

I looked back at "Paris," her blue eyes examining me, not up and down but focusing on my face. She was about my height. Like the other girls in the creative writing class, she was dressed up, wearing a simple white sundress with little pink flowers. It was almost as though she sang springtime and new beginnings. I shook the thought of running through a meadow overflowing with flowers from my head, as the word "Yes" barely escaped my lips. The weight of her hand on my shoulder brought me back to the campus and away from the meadow. "Yes, of course I am," I said. "Why do you ask?"

"Well, you seemed flustered in class. It was the oddest thing. You were completely still, staring at the front of the class for the longest time, until Professor H went up to you. Then you were back. I almost thought you had fallen asleep, only your eyes were wide open."

Now I was feeling anxious, and wishing she would remove her hand from my shoulder. I tried to relax, but all I could feel was her hand on my shoulder, and it was becoming unbearable

"Oh – I was just thinking, that was all. Doesn't everyone space out a little when they are thinking?" I asked, trying to sound casual. "Paris" arched her perfectly groomed eyebrow a little higher, as if she did not believe me.

What was it with people raising their eyebrows at me, I thought? Is it because I'm a freak?

"Anyway, my name is Jane," she said, finally removing her hand from my shoulder and extending it toward me. I looked at her hand before giving it a weak handshake. Her hands were small, soft, and warm. I felt self-conscious, knowing that my hands were cold and clammy.

"My name is, uh, Cathy," I said, quickly pulling my hand away from hers and shoving both hands in my jean pockets.

"I know," she said.

How did she know my name, I thought? I furrowed my forehead desperately, trying to remember when I'd told her my name.

"Don't you remember that Professor H said your name in class?" she said, as she tilted her head to the side.

Now I was really confused.

"Who is Professor H?" I asked.

"Professor Hanson, silly," Jane said with a soft laugh and a flip of her hand off into the air. "I like to call him Professor H since I tend to give people nicknames."

I thought for a moment. Who was the silly one – me or her? But it did make sense. H could stand for so many things like hateful, heartless, and yes, I guess even handsome. I let a small smile break through, and it felt good.

"See, you agree with me," Jane said, as she bumped me with her shoulder.

My smile quickly disappeared when I remembered that I was going to be late for class.

"Hmmm, Jane, it was nice meeting you, but I have to run to my next class," I said, trying to be as pleasant as I could before turning and running down the hallway. I glanced over my shoulder during my jog to see Jane still holding the door and looking at me in disbelief. Why was I so rude to her? I should have been nicer. She was being nice to me; at least I think she was.

What if Jane does like me, I thought? What if Jane wants to be my friend?

I never had a lot of friends growing up. I remember being friends with a group of girls in sixth grade, but that was one of my few attempts to fit in. And I was always getting into trouble whenever I was with them. Sixth grade was not a shining star in my academic career. When sixth grade ended, so did my friendship with the girls.

I had only one girlfriend in high school. If I ever had a best friend, it would have been Charlene, or Char for short. Char and I would study and hang out together. Next to my room, Charlene's house was my other happy place. My friendship with Char ended as soon as we graduated from high school. Charlene had to care for her mom, as I tried to get over mine.

Could it be different this time? Could boring Cathy make friends? The "what ifs" continued spinning in my mind, creating my own little tornado. What if Jane was being nice to me because she liked me? I smiled, cherishing that thought, as I tried to sneak into my biology class without the professor seeing me. I was not successful, since I had to sit in the front row and endure the glares from the professor throughout the long, miserable class. Yes, my first day as a college student was less than stellar.

Chapter Six

The weight of the terrible day quickly disappeared once I shut the front door of my little apartment. I leaned against the door and thought, I'm finally home. Now I am safe. I released the breath that I had been holding since I'd stepped out of my home that morning.

On my way home from my last class, I stopped by an office supply store to buy a few supplies, including a ream of paper. I took the paper out of my backpack and carefully removed its wrapping before placing the stack on my small kitchen table. The table groaned. "Yes, I know your pain," I said, looking at the stack of paper as if it was my enemy. I slowly sat down in the chair, moving the chair closer to the table and closer to the paper. I took a single sheet from the top and placed the blank piece of paper in front of me, its whiteness glaring back at me. I gently slid my hand across the paper, enjoying the feeling. The paper was cool and smooth against my hand. I looked down at the paper, thinking of what I could write about. A flash of seeing Professor Hanson standing behind me brought back an anxious feeling of dread to the pit of my stomach. The bees were starting to wake. I continued to stare at the sheet, just as I had done earlier that day, and once again I could not think of anything to write about. I didn't want to write about me, or who I was. Maybe I was too consumed about who I am and that was causing some type of block, an obstacle I could not overcome.

And what would happen if I'm not able to write, I thought? I bowed my head, letting my forehead rest on the table. If I cannot write about something, I will definitely fail the class. The heaviness of today returned in full force, crushing my body and spirit like a gigantic wave. The urge to cry was overwhelming. I could feel the tears screaming to be released.

I pushed myself away from the table and stumbled over to the couch, sinking myself deep into its soft cushions. I wrapped my arms around myself and closed my eyes. I willed my mind to relax – but a blinding light flashed through my darkness, followed by the large, dark-brown eyes of Professor Hanson. They were glaring at me. I opened my eyes, pushing the vision back and myself up from the softness that was comforting me. I looked to the side of the couch and saw the huge wicker basket I used for storing magazines, junk mail, and various pens. I grabbed a few of the magazines and flipped through them, wondering why I was getting these magazines – Women's Day, Better Homes and Gardens, Sunset. I should really be receiving Cosmo, Shape, or Vogue. I looked at the name on the address label – Betty Pemont. "Hmm, definitely not me," I said out loud – maybe she was the previous tenant.

I turned one page after another, admiring the pictures and articles, while whispering "Who am I." There were pages with beautiful homes, skinny women, happy couples, gorgeous kitchens, thirty-minute meals, and delicious desserts. I saw people biking, hiking, or doing some type of workout. I felt sad and incomplete seeing page after page of happy people doing fun things. I wanted to be someone who biked or hiked and was thin, I thought. Then maybe I would not be so boring.

I let out a heavy sigh, tossing the magazine back into the basket and returning to the blank piece of paper that was patiently waiting for me. Why should I be any different, I thought? I could be someone who biked and hiked and was thin. I sat back in the chair, closed my eyes and dreamt of getting away, of escaping.

Just like the woman in the magazine. I saw myself walking along the beach. I was alone. I could feel the sand between my toes as each step sank into the wet sand. I could hear the water lapping, wave after wave, onto the beach. There were other people on the beach. Some were looking out to the ocean. Some were looking at me. Their stares did not burn into my flesh. Instead, their gazes seemed approving, as if they were in awe of my confidence. I was a different person, gliding down the beach towards a tiny bungalow. The bungalow was nestled among tall palm trees and flowering shrubs. The wind gently stirred the palm fronds. I stopped to look out to the ocean, admiring the moon glistening on the water like an aquatic heaven sparkling with stars. The waves and the wind created a peaceful symphony of sounds. I wrapped my arms around myself and swayed to the harmony that surrounded me. The breeze stirred around my body, bringing a touch of saltiness to my lips. A gentle wave lapped onto the shore and around my feet. The coolness of the water sent tingles from my toes up my legs and to my fingertips. I turned back towards the bungalow to see a single light flickering in the front window. I was being drawn to the light.

My eyes flew open and I started writing. After a few minutes I was amazed at what was in front of me. The page was no longer blank. Instead it was filled with words, line after line of my words. "Yes, Cathy, you can write," I said to myself, giving myself a mental pat on the back.

I pushed myself back in my chair, thinking once again, "Who am I?" After reading what I'd written, I can say that I am a powerful woman, walking down the beach and looking out to the ocean. I am a confident woman walking towards a little bungalow which was my comfortable home. I am waiting for a ship to come to take me away to another adventure. I am a traveler.

I got ready for bed with an overwhelming sense of accomplishment. I had conquered it! The blank page was no longer blank. I closed my eyes, envisioning myself walking on the beach – feeling the sand between my toes and the warm ocean breeze caressing my skin. The sound of the ocean waves breaking on the beach sang a peaceful song that lulled me to sleep.

A blanket of darkness surrounded me. I turned to my right, and then to my left, scanning the horizon. No one was around. I gazed up into the sky to see tiny white specks falling towards me. I stretched my arms out to the side, welcoming the white flakes that were coldly caressing my skin, and began to spin in a slow circle. The gentle breeze I created and the softness of the specks on my skin felt soothing. Both were washing away my fear. Soon I became too dizzy to spin. I stopped, but the room continued to spin. Now the specks became a white wisp, swirling around me. Off to the side I could see a sliver of light, breaking through the sea of darkness. I turned to walk to the light but could not move. My feet and legs were frozen. An uncontrollable shiver took over my body. I rubbed my hands up and down on my arms, trying to warm them, but it was useless. The fear that had disappeared flooded back. The tiny white specks were turning into larger and heavier flakes, each one assaulting my skin. I yanked my legs out of the pile of flakes and ran to the light, hoping to escape the storm. The snowflakes were falling faster and faster, causing the darkness to fade and making it harder for me to find the light. I fought my way through the blizzard, my legs getting heavier and heavier with each step. The sliver of light was now getting bigger. My fears began to subside. And then the light was gone. A tall, shadowy figure stood in front of the light, blocking the light. He did not move. He stood as still as a statue, watching me. Exhaustion and fear won. I could not take another step. I covered myself with my arms, trying to protect myself from the onslaught. I shuddered from the cold, wishing the flakes would stop falling. Even with my eyes closed, I knew the dark figure was watching me withering in the snow. Why doesn't he help me? Can't he see that I am drowning? And why does the dark figure look so familiar? I burst through the mountain of the snow to see that Professor Hanson had disappeared.

I bolted out of bed, my covers wrapped around me. I looked around my bedroom, expecting to see a blanket of snow covering my bed. The only whiteness I saw was that of my sheets. I took a deep breath, trying to calm myself. I instinctively rubbed my arms, thinking they were cold, only to find them extremely warm. I placed my hand on my forehead, feeling the sweat from my latest nightmare. I shook my head, wondering what that dream meant, as I looked at the clock on the nightstand. I moaned, seeing that I had slept in again. "I am going to be late for class," I thought, pushing the covers to the side and jogging to the bathroom to shower.

I thought about the classes that I'd have today while the hot water hit my skin and steam surrounded me. The steam was a lot better than snowflakes, I thought, turning the water off and grabbing a thick towel. Today was psychology, the study of the mind. Boy, did I need someone to study *my* mind! Then again, maybe not, I thought. I'm beginning to think that my mind was a scary place – and what if I determine that I *am* insane?

I threw on some random clothes, and reached for my backpack, when I saw the piece of paper that contained the story I wrote last night. It was still sitting on the table. I picked up the paper, folding it and proudly placing it in the breast pocket of my jean jacket. I thought about the story and wondered why I hadn't dreamt about being on a beach instead of in a snowstorm. Yep, I'm going to learn I'm insane, I thought, grabbing my backpack and keys.

I was pulling out of the parking lot of the apartment complex, when I realized I was in such a hurry this morning that I hadn't asked my question. Nothing seemed out of the ordinary. Maybe I should reevaluate my sad ritual. "Who am I?" I said out loud as I drove to campus. "Someone who is going to be late for class if she doesn't stop talking to herself," I said out loud.

Chapter Seven

It was a quick drive to campus. Even with the late start, I thought I must be lucky today since there wasn't much traffic, and I got an excellent parking spot without having to drive around in circles. I mentally thanked my guardian angel as I jerked the car into "park" and jumped out of the car.

I dashed to the classroom, dragging my backpack and butt across the plaza. I had to thank my guardian angel again, since I did not have to dodge a sea of students to get to class. But was it because of my guardian angel or the fact that I was probably late for class? I sucked in a deep breath before willing my legs to move a little faster, praying that I would not be late.

I came to an abrupt stop at the entrance to the classroom, gasping for air and scanning the huge classroom for an empty chair. My heart sank when I saw that there were only a few empty chairs, and most were in the front. I did a quick glance to the back row to see that there were two empty seats, and they were in the middle of the row. I was not going to ask anyone to get up so that I could pass them. I dropped my head, bringing my chin to my chest, and reluctantly took a seat in the front. The professor was already busy writing on the board.

The class never seemed to end as the ticking of the clocking slowed and the back of my neck burned. I looked around to find out who was staring at me, only to see that everyone was listening to the professor. I was turning back to the front of the class when I saw Jane sitting in the middle of the classroom. The class just got a little better, knowing that Jane was in it too. Jane saw me and smiled. I smiled back, giving her a slight wave instead of a confused look.

Class finally ended, and I'm not certain what the professor had discussed. My mind kept returning to my dream, wondering what it meant, and why Professor Hanson was a part of that dream. Maybe the psychology class will have a section on analyzing dreams, I thought, as I closed my book and grabbed my backpack. I stood up, getting ready to leave, when I heard my name. I turned and saw Jane coming towards me with the biggest smile I had ever seen.

"Hi, Jane," I said, trying to match her smile but knowing that it was hopeless. I had never met anyone so happy and full of life before.

"Cathy, I am so excited that we have another class together. Do you have time to get some coffee? I know of this cute little coffee shop just a block from campus. I've been dying to try it," she asked, moving in very close to me as if she would pounce on me if I said no.

I started to decline her invitation, and then I thought, why not? It would be good for me to make a new friend, and Jane was nice. Her kindness was still catching me off guard. I had an hour before my next class, which should be plenty of time to get coffee, I thought. I'd been planning to hang out at the library until my next class, but hanging out with Jane sounded more exciting.

"Sure," I said with a smile. At least it felt like a smile to me.

"Awesome!" she said. "The place is just a few blocks away." She turned and moved quickly down the hallway. I followed obediently, trying to keep pace with her tap, tap, tap, which should not have been hard since I was wearing running shoes and Jane was not. How does she walk so fast in heels?

Jane continued to chat, and I continued to listen, as we made our way across the campus and to the coffee shop. I was wishing I could be as sociable, confident, and happy as Jane. How does she do it, I thought? She makes it seem so easy, almost effortless.

We got to the coffee shop and it was crowded. My heart sank, thinking that we would have to stand to drink our coffee. Jane was right; the coffee shop was the place to be. Jane nudged her way through the crowd and I followed. We were able to find a small table with two cushy chairs off in a secluded corner. I plopped down with relief and enjoyed the softness of the chair. It reminded me of my couch at home. The packed coffee shop was buzzing with conversation, as everyone was discussing their classes, which professors they liked, and which ones were tough. I was holding a huge mug of coffee close to my nose, letting the warmth seep into my hands. I closed my eyes and inhaled the rich coffee aroma that encircled the mug, and thought that I was in heaven. I opened my eyes just in time to observe Jane pouring three packets of sugar and a splash of half-and-half into her coffee. I watched as she gently stirred the contents in her mug. I felt as though I was watching a commercial for Folgers. Jane was so pretty and precise, as she stirred for what seemed to be several minutes. Perhaps I was lost in time, sipping my coffee, and struggling to think of something to say.

Jane finally finished stirring her coffee, as she gently tapped the tiny spoon on the top of her mug and placed it on top of a white paper napkin next to her mug. She sat back on her cushioned chair, bringing the mug to her glossy, pink lips and taking a sip of her coffee concoction. I was absorbed with each move she made. She was fluid – almost as if she were floating in front of my eyes.

The silence was now hanging over us as I asked myself what to say, what to say. I took another drink, looking away from Jane and out the window that was next to our table. More students were flooding into the coffee shop. I had to wonder where they would sit since the little coffee shop was already packed.

"What do you think of Professor H?" Jane asked, as if she were inquiring about the weather.

I almost choked on my coffee. I don't know if it was because she snapped me back from my daydream, or the fact that she mentioned Professor H.

"He seems too young and definitely too cute to be a professor," I blurted out. "And what's with the icy cold stares? I have to wonder if he is human." I rushed to put my hands over my mouth. I was shocked by my forward response. I think Jane was also surprised.

"Cathy, you are pretty funny," she said with a giggle.

I didn't know what to think of that remark. How can I be funny? I am not funny. Maybe she thinks I'm "funny odd."

"Why do you say I'm funny?" I asked defensively.

"Oh, I don't know. You are so quiet. Most of my girlfriends talk a lot – and I mean a *lot*. Yet they never have much to say. You are interesting in that you are so quiet one minute, and then you blurt out something funny just seconds later."

I had to think about this. I assumed she'd just given me a compliment.

"Jane, I have to ask you something that has been nagging me since we first met." I paused, gathering some courage and the right words.

"Yessss?" Jane asked, drawing out the "s" in an effort to coax the question out of me.

"Why did you say "hi" to me, or even smile at me in class yesterday?" There, I said it. I swallowed in fear, wondering what her response would be.

Jane sat back in her chair, taking another drink of her coffee concoction and pondering my question. Well, it seemed to me that she was pondering. Maybe she was trying to look for the right words to say without offending me.

"I don't know – you just seemed different. I always like different." She responded as if the question was not a big deal. "I also sensed some type of connection between us. I mean, haven't you ever been drawn to someone and you didn't know why? Sometimes people arrive in your life at just the right time. You don't understand why. It just feels right, almost like being wrapped in your favorite blanket or drinking hot coffee in a comfortable chair." Jane peeked over the edge of her coffee mug with a sly grin after sharing her theory.

I had to wonder if Jane had spiked her coffee with something a little stronger than half-and-half. Connection – how can we have a connection when we'd just met? Okay, connection. I don't get it, but I will go along with it. And a person coming into your life at the right time without a reasonable explanation? I was having a hard time understanding that concept. Yet, I had to admit that having Jane enter my life was good, and unexplainable. I sat back in my chair, letting the warmth from my coffee mug and Jane's connection radiate through my body and swirl in my mind. A weight had instantly been removed after asking Jane why she had been so nice to me, but there was another question that I had to ask. I placed my coffee mug down and moved to the edge of the thick-cushioned chair, bringing me closer to Jane.

"Jane," I said slowly. "I've told you what *I* think of Professor H. I've been wondering what *you* think of him. I can't be the only one who thinks he is good looking."

A huge smile cracked through Jane's perfect porcelain complexion.

"Oh! I think Professor H is extremely dreamy. The only reason I'm taking the class is because of him. I wish he was teaching more classes," Jane said as she looked up to the ceiling – almost as if she were looking into the clouds and seeing his face.

I was a little shocked by her answer, and wondered if she remembered that I was still sitting across from her as she went on and on about him.

"Don't you think he is a little young to be a professor? He must be, what, thirty?" I asked.

"Thirty sounds about right, but I know a number of professors who are around that age. It doesn't really matter. I just hope he stays around after this semester," Jane said, in a distant voice. She must still be stuck in the clouds, I thought. I was curious about her last comment.

"Jane, why wouldn't Professor H stay around? Hasn't he been teaching for a while?"

Jane moved closer to the table as if she was going to tell me a secret that she did not want anyone else to hear. I'm not certain if I found her demeanor amusing or exciting. I automatically followed her lead as I also inched closer to Jane.

"This is the first semester that Professor H is teaching at this college. I heard that he was a tenured professor at a prominent university. I'm not certain why he left, but I don't think it was under good circumstances. I am definitely going to find out what happened." I could mentally see Jane putting her detective hat on as she tapped her finger to her chin.

I was surprised and somewhat disappointed that Professor H was new to the area. I swore he looked familiar, but if he had just moved here, I must have him confused with some movie star – or maybe he just looks like someone I once knew. I glanced down at my cell phone to see that my next class was going to be starting in ten minutes. A wave of panic pushed away my warm and happy feeling. I did not want to be late for another class. I grabbed the mug, which was now cold, and cringed as I swallowed the last of the coffee. There was nothing worse than cold coffee, I thought.

"Hey Jane," I said, pushing myself out of the chair. "I need to run to my next class. It was great chatting with you." I picked up my backpack off the scuffed wooden floor and ran to the door of the coffee shop. Once again I was being rude since I was quickly leaving. I glanced back at Jane before shoving the door open, to see a somewhat confused look on Jane's pretty face. Yes, I was right, I am rude. I had to wonder if she was going to reconsider her comment about having a connection with me as I turned back around and rushed through the door. Maybe there was something worse than cold coffee, I thought, as I jogged towards campus. A rude friend was definitely worse.

Chapter Eight

I stopped in front of the doors leading to my business class, relieved to see that I was not late. My heart was beating out of my chest, either from running or from fear of being late. It was probably both. I walked to the back of the classroom, sucking in a deep breath and slowly letting it out, as I perched myself in the last row and watched the rest of the students fill the room. It was nice to see that there were a fairly equal number of girls and boys, and that they were dressed just like me in jeans and t-shirt.

A tall, slender guy with brown, wavy hair walked into the classroom. My breath caught in my throat. I've seen that guy before, I thought, but where? My mind was frantically trying to remember where and when. He was good looking, just like Professor H, but more human rather than cold like a statue. Like the other students, he wore faded jeans. Like me, he was wearing a jean jacket. I discreetly watched him walk up the aisle and towards the back of the class. My heart resumed its erratic beating as he moved closer and closer towards me. I looked down at my notebook, hoping that he did not see me gawking at him, and silently praying that he did not sit next to me. I glanced up and released the breath I was holding. He was moving down a row in the middle of the classroom where a bunch of guys were sitting. He must know them, I thought, since the guys looked up in recognition. Just before turning to take his seat, he looked to the back of the room and noticed me noticing him. Our eyes locked. My heart stopped its erratic beating. He brushed his hand through his brown, wavy hair and smiled. I couldn't help but smile back as my heart resumed beating – but it was more of a fluttering as if I had just swallowed a butterfly. The tall guy's smile got bigger and his eyes crinkled with amusement. He turned to the group of guys, patting one guy on the back as if they were best friends. The other guy said something, maybe his name, but I couldn't hear what he said. Now I was mentally kicking myself for sitting in the back.

The professor walked in, snapping my focus and my posture back to the classroom and away from the tall, cute guy. My rigid body eased when I saw that the professor was a woman, and not a good-looking man. I was also thankful that she wasn't writing questions on the board about who we were and what we would like to aspire to. Throughout the class, I switched my attention to the top of the tall guy's head, and to Professor Gautier, wondering if the tall, good-looking guy could feel my gaze. And then the mental debate ensued. Why did he smile at me? Maybe it was just an automatic reaction when you catch someone looking at you, or maybe he's a nice guy. He seemed very friendly with his buddies. I'm certain that was it. He's a nice guy.

Between my mental debates, my frequent glances in the direction of the tall guy, and the topic, class quickly ended. I was surprised that I enjoyed the parts of the class that I did hear. Yes, I do believe this will be my favorite class, I thought. I'm not certain if it was because of the tall, good-looking guy, the topic, or both. I stayed in my seat, rather than bolting for the doorway, once Professor Gautier excused the class. I did not want to take the chance of bumping into the tall, cute guy. Staying behind was the safest thing for me to do. I watched the tall, good-looking guy leave the classroom with his buddies. I was a little disappointed that he was busy talking to his friends, rather than looking my way, when he left. Yes, he was just being nice, I thought. I did not have another class to rush off to, so I sat back and waited until the last student left the classroom. The professor was placing the last of her papers into her briefcase when she noticed me and smiled. I smiled back. Like the tall, good-looking guy, the professor had a nice smile that made me like the class even more. I pushed myself up from the desk and walked down the aisle, thinking that maybe I will be a business executive when I grow up.

I left the empty classroom to an equally empty hallway. No one was running to class or milling around. The hallway was dim and quiet. I was disappointed that the tall guy was not waiting for me. But seriously, why should he, I thought? He was just being friendly and nothing more. I strolled down the hallway, listening to how each footstep echoed off the red-brick walls. The light at the end of the hallway was just like the light in both of my dreams. At least I knew that the plaza was on the other side of the door, and not my reflection, or Professor Hanson. I pushed the doors open, letting the cool breeze sweep through my hair and brush against my cheeks. It was a beautiful September day. The breeze was also causing the red and orange leaves to dance across the plaza. I was mesmerized by their movement, as if the leaves were having their own race, with each leaf having its turn being in the lead, and the breeze coming along from time to time to kick the leaves up into the air. I followed the leaves as they twirled towards the blue sky. I noticed there was not a single cloud to be read, just a blanket of blue suspended above me. I stood looking up to the sky, letting the sun touch my cheeks. I closed my eyes and smiled, thinking about the tall, good-looking guy with the nice smile and the brown, wavy hair. What if *he* thought *I* was cute?

Oh seriously, Cathy, I thought to myself, get a grip. Why would he be interested in you? He was just being nice. I let out a heavy sigh, knowing that my inner voice was right – he was just being nice. I resumed my stroll across the campus and towards the parking lot. To the right of the plaza I saw a small group of guys laughing and talking. I could only make out a few words, like "business," "practice," and "game." I glanced at the group and noticed the tall, good-looking guy towering above the other guys. And once again, my breath caught in my throat. I peeked to the side instead of looking at him, praying that I would not trip. I could tell that he saw me, and I could feel his head following me, as I continued my trek to the parking lot. My heart was beating in time with each step. I reached the driver's side of my car and turned to face the plaza. The group of guys looked like a shadowy mass with little distinction. The only thing I could make out was the tall, good-looking guy, and he was looking in my direction. My heart jumped. He extended his arm up and waved. My hand automatically reached to the sky and waved back, only to see both his wave and him morph into the shadowy mass.

Chapter Nine

I arrived at work, my cheeks aching. While I love my job at the pillow factory, the real reason for my continuous smile was because of him – the tall, good-looking guy. I played the scene of him smiling and waving to me over and over in my mind while I drove to work. Still, I was happy to be at work, since that meant I would see Fred. Fred was my shift supervisor and the closest thing I had to a dad – well, really, a grandfather. Fred was an older man with a gray beard. What hair he had was also gray. Fred reminded me of Santa Claus because he was a little overweight, very jolly, and fond of sugar cookies – but then again, who doesn't like sugar cookies.

I pulled open the heavy metal door that led to the breakroom and served as the employees' entrance. I blinked my eyes several times, adjusting to the dim light. Even the fluorescent lights did little in illuminating the bleakness of the breakroom. The one thing that did brighten the room was Fred, and he was sitting at a table reading a newspaper. He looked up after hearing the metal door shut, and beamed. I smiled back, feeling a little lighter and a lot more relaxed. Any bad feelings I had were quickly washed away whenever Fred smiled at me. I was thinking it was a shame that I hadn't seen Fred after my creative writing class, and the mishap with the stony Professor H.

Fred pushed himself up from the table and moved towards me. I jogged over to him and gave him a big hug, letting his cheerfulness flow into my body and making me feel happy and at ease. Strange that when I am at work, I can feel like I've finally come home. After hugging Fred, I went over to the changing room to put on the usual attire for working in the packaging section of the pillow factor – gloves, overalls, and safety glasses – all the stylish items any woman would want to wear. I had to wonder if Jane would ever be caught dead wearing anything that resembled overalls. Perhaps if they were made of leather, I thought.

Fred returned to his paper, engrossed in an article, by the time I'd returned to the breakroom. Fred looked up from the paper when he heard the creak of the door that was between the breakroom and changing room. He smiled as if he'd just seen me for the first time that day.

"Cathy, I've been anxious to hear about your classes. Do you like being a college student?" Fred asked, as he neatly folded the paper and placed it to the side.

I returned to the round table and sat down in one of the metal chairs that surrounded it. I was excited and a little scared to share my first week of being a college student with Fred. I knew I did not want to talk about the Assignment from Hell or Professor H.

"I've decided that I'm not fond of psychology, but I really like my business class," I said with a smile. Fred nodded his head in approval, with his smile spreading wider in his chubby face.

"And it seems I've made a new friend. Her name is Jane, and she is very pretty. I'm not sure why she wants to be my friend, though," I added with a heavy sigh, looking down at the beige table and avoiding Fred's blue-gray eyes.

"Now, now, Cathy, anyone would be lucky to have you as a friend," Fred said, placing his hands on top of mine. The warmth from his hands was soothing. "I'm glad you finally listened to the doctor and decided to move on with your life. There's more to life than this place and your tiny apartment. Going to college will be just what you needed," he added with a touch of concern and a twinkle in his eyes.

I guess that was an interesting way of saying what the doctor had ordered, I thought. I hadn't thought of or seen Doc in weeks. I pushed myself away from the table before Fred could ask about the Doc. While I enjoyed talking to Fred, and he seemed to know the right thing to say at the right time, I was not ready to talk about the Doc. I gave Fred a quick hug before reporting to my shift, thankful that Fred turned his attention back to his paper rather than keeping it on me.

The first week of classes ended, and I was physically and emotionally exhausted. A lot of memories surfaced during the week, and most were painful. I stood in front of the bathroom mirror, looking to see if I had changed in any way. The same hazel eyes were staring back at me, only now, the dark circles were fading into a very tired face. "Who am I" came back with a sudden force. I could feel the heat in my cheeks as I thought of Professor Hanson standing next to me, waiting for me to finish the Assignment from Hell. I hit my forehead on the mirror in frustration. He probably thinks I'm an idiot. Yes, that's who I am – an idiot. I could feel the butterflies awaken in my stomach as I thought of the tall, good-looking guy with brown, wavy hair.

I pushed myself away from the bathroom sink and walked to the kitchen to find the stack of paper sitting on the table. The paper was calling to me, in that constant hum that I've grown so accustomed to. I sat down on the chair, hearing the chair groan from my weight. I ran my hand across the stack before removing the top sheet and placing it in front of me. The paper was staring at me, just the way it did a few days ago. I closed my eyes but could still see the whiteness of the paper glaring back at me, almost mocking me. I let my head rest on the small kitchen table. The coolness from the table felt inviting and soothing to my forehead. I started thinking of snow. The paper reminded me of the snow on the ground after a blizzard. My mind continued to drift, and soon the two-year-old that I could not remember surfaced. She did not have a face but I knew it was a girl, since she was wearing a simple white dress with blue trim. I smiled. I could see the hint of bruises on her knees from falling. The little girl reached out for me. I reached for her, but then I saw a woman scooping the little girl into her arms. I watched the woman swing the little girl in a circle. They were both laughing. I could feel my smile getting bigger and bigger, almost to the point of hurting my face. My eyes swelled with tears, because I knew that the two-year old was me and the woman was Mom.

I woke up the next morning to find the piece of paper plastered to my face. I had fallen asleep in the small kitchen chair, and my back was aching. I pulled the paper from my cheek and placed it back on the table. I stumbled to the bathroom and splashed cold water on my face, my face and hands tingling from the icy water. I gazed into the mirror to see that the dark circles had returned. I looked worse than ever, I thought, pushing myself away from the mirror without asking my question. I was too tired to ask that silly question – and really, I already knew the answer, so why waste my time.

I dragged my tired and aching body back to the kitchen. I needed a cup of strong coffee. I moved from the refrigerator to the coffee pot and stopped in disbelief when I saw the crinkled page on the kitchen table. The page was no longer blank, but filled with many words and lines. I lowered myself to the chair and read the words that I had written:

There was a little girl wearing a white dress trimmed with blue standing alone at the edge of the playground. A gentle breeze swung her white dress around, causing the dress to puff out around her tiny body. She scanned the playground, looking for her mother among the other mothers, who were scattered among the swings, slides, and monkey bars. Some mothers were smiling as they swung their little ones around in a circle. Some mothers were chasing after their children, both of them giggling.

The little girl saw a woman off in the distance. The little girl thought that the woman must be her mother. She was not chasing anyone. She was not pushing anyone in the swing. The little girl cried out "Mom," hoping to get the woman's attention. The woman turned to the little girl. At first the little girl thought the woman would run to her, giving her a big hug and swinging her in a circle. But the woman turned back around and drifted into the dark forest that surrounded the playground. The little girl ran towards the woman. That has to be my mom, the little girl thought. The little girl cried out "Mom, Mom" as she ran faster and faster towards the woman. But the woman continued to walk away from the little girl, disappearing into the dark forest. The girl was too tired to run any more. She stopped, falling onto her knees, and started crying. The little girl was confused. Mom, why did you leave me? The little girl cried into her hands, with the sand and gravel from the playground digging into her knees.

Tears streamed down my cheeks and my heart sank. That was not the dream I'd had last night. That dream was a happy dream with the two-year-old girl in the arms of a young woman. They were swinging, dancing, and laughing together. But that was not what the paper said. I let go of the paper, letting it slowly drift down to the floor with a loud thud. I'm not certain if the sound was from the paper or from my heart. I was sad and confused.

I looked at the clock to see that I had less than an hour to make it to class. I let out a moan before running to the bedroom and throwing on my usual attire of jeans and a T-shirt. I jogged back to the kitchen, picking up the piece of paper from the floor and tucking it into my backpack, before rushing out of the apartment and to my car.

I was still able to get to class before Jane. I was hoping to talk to her before class, but Jane was not one for getting to class early. I smiled and waved as she walked in. She waved back, taking a seat near the front of the classroom. My heart sank a little when she decided not to sit next to me. Maybe she was mad at me for leaving the coffee shop in such a hurry. Then again, if she sat in the back with me, she would not have as good a view of Professor H.

The abrupt silence pulled me back and signaled that Professor H had just entered the classroom. I could see Jane sit an inch taller, with all her attention focused on him. Of course, Jane was not the only one. Every head followed him as he sauntered to the front of the room. He sat on the edge of his desk and scanned the classroom. The silence in the room got thicker with each passing second. Students were inching closer to the edge of their chairs, anxiously waiting for Professor H to speak. His steady gaze had the opposite effect on me. I leaned back in my chair, hoping to escape his view. He coughed into his hand, clearing his throat. A few students jumped from the sound.

"Class, I want to talk to you about your first assignment. There were some interesting papers that showed potential, and then there were some that were unusual and basically incomplete." His cold voice drifted outward into the classroom.

I'm certain he looked at me when he said the words "unusual and incomplete." The temperature in the room must have increased at least ten degrees, causing beads of sweat to form on my forehead. Professor H pushed himself off the desk and paced from one side of the classroom to the other, with each head automatically following him. He moved back to the center of the room and stopped looking out into the classroom.

"I want each one of you to ask yourself why you are taking this class. If you are not serious about the subject, then I highly recommend that you drop the class now," Professor H said, this time with an authoritative tone echoing in the classroom. The chill I felt when he was standing behind me on the first day of classes returned. I quietly moved, wrapping my jean jacket around my shoulders in hopes of bringing some warmth into my body.

The heavy silence was being etched away as a few of the students sitting next to one another started to mumble, trying to understand why he'd just said what he did. I too was confused. Why accuse the entire classroom when the harsh statements were meant just for me, I thought?

Professor H turned his back to the classroom and wrote something on the board. I sensed that the classroom was afraid, since the muttering had faded and all eyes once again focused on his every move. The class seemed more attentive than usual, though it was hard to imagine that Professor H could gain any more attention than he normally did. I gazed down at my notebook, focusing on the cruel words he'd just spoken rather than the words that were now coming out of his mouth. The class was dragging and my mind drifted. I was certain that the icy voice of Professor H had frozen time. My mind was too occupied with the words "unusual" and "incomplete" to hear anything else that was leaving his lips. I noticed that I had written those words several times in my notebook. I flipped the notebook over to hide the words, and to keep them from taunting me. I shifted my focus to Jane and the apology she deserved. I should probably apologize to Professor H too, but the thought of confronting his icy voice and statue-like stance brought fear and nausea to the pit of my stomach.

The class finally ended with Professor H giving us another writing assignment. I was relieved that I would be able to do this assignment on my own, rather than in class. I closed my notebook, getting ready to call out Jane's name, when Professor H called out my name first. I froze, unable to move. It felt as though the carpet had turned into thick mud, and I was stuck in place.

All eyes went from him to me. I had to wonder if there was a hint of jealousy behind some of the stares. All I could think of was that he was going to ask me to drop the class or stay after class to redo the Assignment from Hell. Isn't that what had happened to me several times in high school?

Jane's gaze followed me as I found some way to move my feet down the aisle to the front of the classroom. I looked at her and mouthed "I have to talk to you" as I slowly passed by. She nodded and said okay. That was a good sign, I thought.

I stopped at the side of his desk, waiting for the room to empty. It was minutes before I could no longer hear the whispers or the shuffling of students' feet. Silence surrounded me. I swallowed, trying to find the courage to speak.

"Hmmm, you wanted to see me, Professor Hanson?" I squeaked out.

Professor H cleared his voice before saying "Cathy."

He did not move, but stayed behind the desk. I blew out a sigh, knowing that the desk separated us. I propped the side of my body onto the desk just in case I fainted. Nauseous fear was now rumbling in my stomach and echoing in my head. I seriously thought I was going to get sick. I kept my eyes fixated on the beige carpet, since I knew I did not have the courage to look at his stony face.

"I am a little concerned that this class may not be right for you," he continued. "You seem to have a problem writing a simple request. If you cannot complete a simple assignment, I do not see how you would be able to continue with this class. Remember what I said in class – if you are not serious about the topic, then you should drop the class now."

His words hit me like a hard punch to my gut. I sucked in my breath and grabbed onto the desk. I clutched my fingers on the edge of the desk. I could feel the blood flow out of my fingers as I gripped the desk tighter and tighter. Soon the throbbing in my knuckles became excruciating, but it paled in comparison to the pain that his words were inflicting on me. I swallowed hard, trying to find something to say, some reply to his awful statement. I kept my gaze down. I didn't want Professor H to see the hurt I was feeling. But then I had to wonder if he really cared that his words were so hurtful.

I knew he was waiting for me to say something, but seriously, what do you say when a professor has just told you that you are not good enough to be in his class? I felt as if I was back in the corner of my room, watching Mom as she tore my room apart, my heart breaking with every treasure she threw on the floor and every poster she ripped off the wall. Only this time, each spiteful word he uttered felt like a sharp, cold blade digging deep into the pit of my stomach. I brought my mind back to the classroom and to Professor H. He was still waiting for me to say something.

Once again I had to ask, "Who am I," and Professor H had just said that I was not a writer. Do I really have what it takes to be a college student, I thought? My self-doubt was coming back in full force. I thought I had pushed back my insecurities, but I was wrong. I frantically blinked back the tears that were threatening. I'm not certain if the tears were because of what Professor H had said, or because of the memories that were rushing back.

The silence was getting heavier and heavier with each passing second. Professor H broke the silence by clearing his throat again. I was beginning to hate him, and his habit of clearing his throat.

"I know what I said may be a little harsh, but I do not want you to be wasting your time or mine."

A *little* harsh, I thought? More like a *lot*. There was no end to his cruelty. I had to wonder if all good-looking men were as callous as Professor H. It was my turn to clear my throat. My mind was desperately trying to find something to say.

"I was surprised by the questions," I finally whispered.

I swallowed again before saying why it was so hard for me to share anything about my life, about me. Do I really have to share it with him? I know I didn't want to. Maybe I could make something up, just the way I did a few nights ago.

"Yes, you're right to question my abilities," I said, my voice wavering. "I'm not certain if I'm meant to be a writer." I took another gulp of air, slightly lifting my head in his direction, but keeping my focus on his chin rather than his eyes. "I'm not certain what I am meant to do, but I thought it would be a good class for me to discover what I *could* be."

Wow, I thought that was good. I had to think he thought so too, since his jaw clenched. Maybe he was surprised that I did not agree with him. I'm certain few people would argue with Professor H.

"I see," he said, almost drawing the two words out longer than they should be.

More silence. I guess that was better than another harsh remark, or another clearing of his throat, I thought.

I remembered the piece of paper that had captured my dreams of being a traveler. I had placed that piece of paper in the pocket of my jean jacket a few days ago. I also remembered the piece of paper that captured the story of the little girl looking for her mother on the playground. That story was secretly tucked away in my backpack. I could not give him that piece of paper. I pulled the folded piece of paper from the pocket of my jean jacket.

"Professor Hanson, after the last assignment that I failed miserably at, I decided to practice the assignment at home. I wrote this the other night."

My hand was shaking as I handed him the folded piece of paper. I wasn't sure why my hand was shaking. I know I did not enjoy standing in front of him as he questioned my abilities. I know the story of being a traveler doesn't really answer the Assignment from Hell. I finally realized why my hand was shaking when I let my eyes meet his. He scared me. My knees were shaky, just as they were when I was getting ready to sing my solo during the Christmas pageant. Yep, I'm going to get sick, I thought. I returned my grip to the desk, hoping to steady myself and my stomach.

"Hopefully this will be better than my first attempt," I whispered, returning my gaze to the desk.

He looked down at the paper and began to unfold it, letting the words and the lines flourish. I took a chance to glance at him while he looked at the paper. I swear I saw a small smile break through the stern mask he always seemed to be wearing. I fought back the urge to smile, but I did mentally pat myself on the back.

"I will take a look at it over the weekend," he said. "Do not forget to work on the next assignment," he added, as he tucked the paper into his briefcase. He may have cracked a small smile, but his voice did not get any warmer.

I turned, not saying another word, and rushed away from him. I didn't think I could have gotten out of the classroom any quicker. I wanted my legs to move faster, but they felt like lead. I pushed open the door, sucking in the air that he had kicked out of me. The fresh air was soothing. I leaned against the wall, willing my breath to return. I'm such a failure, I thought. The hallway was humming with students walking to their next class. I closed my eyes listening to the hum, and thinking that I was going to be late for class if I did not start walking.

I heard my name, which caused my heart to skip. Ugh, that cannot be Professor H, I thought. I couldn't take any more of his vicious statements and icy scowls. I turned to see that it was Jane. If she was mad at me, it must have passed. Jane walked up to me and placed her hand lightly on my shoulder.

"Are you okay, Cathy?" she asked gently, stepping a little closer to me.

I had to laugh, since it seemed she was always asking me that question. *"Am* I okay?" I had to ask myself.

I moaned before telling Jane what Professor H had said to me. I was surprised that I did not break down in tears. Instead, relief washed over me as I shared every hateful and cruel word that Professor H had uttered.

"Wow," she said in amazement, "that was harsh!"

"That's what I thought," I said. "Maybe he's right; maybe I'm not meant to be a writer. I should drop the class and stop wasting my time and his," I said, feeling defeated and incredibly sad.

Saying the words out loud seemed to bring finality to the issue. "Stop wasting your time, Cathy," I repeated to myself. I should just go back to my little apartment and hide underneath my blue comforter.

"Oh Cathy, who cares if you were not meant to be a writer; you can still take the class. You just have to figure out what to write about. Let your imagination soar," Jane said, as if it were no big deal.

"I think that's my problem, Jane. I am not very imaginative. Anyway, I have to run to my next class. I think I'm already late. Oh, and Jane, I'm sorry about leaving in such a hurry yesterday. You were being very nice to me, and I'm just not used to it. Can we get together tonight, or maybe tomorrow?" I asked.

I don't know what surprised Jane more, the fact that I said I was sorry or that I wanted to get together. I'm not certain which was bigger, the smile on her face or her blue eyes.

"Sure, that would be great! I was going to happy hour later this afternoon at a pub that's a few blocks away from campus. Are you interested?" she asked, almost with a little hop. Yes, I think I did surprise her, and it made me happy.

A pub, I thought to myself. That meant drinking. I was hoping for coffee. I was not a big drinker, but I really did need to push myself out of my comfort zone.

"Sure, that would be great," I said, trying to plaster a big smile on my face and hoping that I did not come off as plastic or nervous.

Jane and I exchanged phone numbers and planned a time when we would meet.

I ran off to my next class, only to have to sit in the front again. I hoped the professor did not hear the "ugh" escaping from my mind when I sat down. I had to wonder if he did, since he glared at me when I pulled my notebook and pen out of my backpack and forced myself to focus on the professor discussing the wonderful world of the ecosystem.

Chapter Ten

It was easy to find the pub. Of course, I got there before Jane. The inside of the pub was dark and musty, with an earthy smell hitting my nose once I walked inside. The pub was not as crowded as the little coffee shop Jane and I had gone to last week. There were a few guys sitting by themselves at the bar, hunched over a pint of beer. The only sounds were music droning throughout the pub and the occasional sound of glass landing on the metal top of the bar with a distinct clink.

The last time I was at a pub was when the Doc convinced me to do something other than spending another evening alone in my tiny apartment. So I pulled myself out of my self-induced despair and joined a few of my co-workers for a going-away party. I definitely felt out of place as the ladies from work were drinking, talking about work, and checking out the guys. I spent most of my time sipping on a light beer and watching my co-workers ogling the guys, and the guys examining them right back. I had to wonder who was going to make the first move. The ladies at work would loudly whisper that the one with the plaid shirt was hot or the one in the black T-shirt reminded her of her ex-boyfriend. A few connections were made that night. I never asked if they lasted.

One guy did capture my attention. Like the tall, good-looking guy, he had brown, wavy hair. And like Professor H, he wore wire-framed glasses. He was sitting at the bar with a few other guys. He was definitely good looking, since a number of my co-workers told me so. He and I made eye contact and smiled at each other a couple of times throughout the evening. One co-worker noticed our visual exchange and tried to get me to go over to talk to him. I laughed. Whatever courage I'd mustered to push myself out of my apartment and to the bar had already been exhausted. His buddies must have noticed our exchange, since they were prodding him to go over to talk to me. He never did. I left the bar that night a little disappointed, but knowing deep down inside he would never be interested in someone like me.

And there I stood again, in the middle of a bar, questioning both my existence in this place and my next action. I was glad that the few guys sitting at the bar were focused on their beer, rather than gawking at me. I found a table in the corner that was just across from the entrance into the pub. I sat facing the door so that Jane could see me when she came in. The wooden chairs were not as comfortable as the cushy chairs at the coffee shop. I sipped water, scanning the pub and thinking it would be funny if I did see that guy with the wavy hair and wire-framed glasses. Maybe I should write about that in my next assignment. Now that would get Professor H's attention, I thought. And then it hit me. Professor H has wavy hair and wears wire-framed glasses. I had to wonder if Professor H was the guy that I was sharing glances with the last time I was at a bar. But then I remembered Jane saying that Professor H was new to town, so he could not have been the same guy. Not to mention that I don't think the stoic Professor H would be human enough to share a visual exchange with anyone – let alone me.

I heard my name, floating with the drone of some song, to see Jane frantically waving and snapping me back to the pub. Jane really did not need to yell my name to get my attention.

Jane walking into the room would grab anyone's attention. She was stunning, almost as if she had been plucked out of a fashion magazine and dropped inside the pub. Jane was dressed in a crisp white shirt, leather leggings, and boots. Her jewelry was always simple, silver or gold hoops depending on the necklace she was wearing. I was in awe. How can Jane make the simple look so fabulous? It must be her smile, I thought. Jane's smile can light up a room, causing all heads to turn, and they did. Just as when Professor H had walked into the room on the first day of class. Yet it was odd how they both exuded confidence – but how differently I perceived them. With Jane it seemed as though she was naïve about her confidence; it was simply a natural part of her existence. With Professor H, it felt as though he used his confidence to intimidate people – at least his students, or maybe just me.

Jane gracefully sat in the wooden seat across from me and waved for the waitress to come over. Jane always seemed to be in command. I sat back watching the scene, just as if I were watching a movie.

"What would you like to drink, Cathy? This round is on me."

What to drink, what to drink? I asked myself.

My mom never drank and we never had liquor in our house. My earliest memory of drinking was when I would go to Char's house for a sleepover. Her mom was so cool. She would let us drink 7-Up and amaretto. I got a little drunk one time, which meant I almost finished one drink. My mom found out the next day and grounded me for a month. Drinking was never the same after that.

"Hellooo," Jane said, snapping her fingers in front of my face. "What would you like to drink?" she asked again.

"Oh, sorry. I'll have a light beer," I whispered, since the memory of being grounded was still fresh.

Jane looked at me as if I'd just ordered water.

"Are you on a diet or something?" she asked.

"No!" I responded, looking down at myself and wondering if I *should* be on a diet.

"Should I be on a diet?" I asked.

"Of course not, silly, you look great! I wish I was as tall as you."

I had to wonder if we were looking at the same person. I look great? I look boring – that's what I looked like. And Jane and I were the same height, since I can look directly into her blue eyes whenever we're standing in front of each another. Then again, she was always wearing high heels.

"Cathy, don't you think you're pretty?" she asked. It was almost as if she could read my mind.

"No, I think I look plain, just like a plain Jane." Ugh. I'd done it again. The words had escaped from my mouth before I knew what I was saying.

"Oh, I'm sorry, Jane," I quickly added, once I knew the words were out. "You are *far* from being plain!" I blew out a heavy sigh, letting my shoulders sag. I felt like a terrible friend, calling Jane plain.

Jane laughed.

"Oh, Cathy, I'm not upset. I get the impression that you don't think much of yourself. I believe you lack self-confidence," Jane said, as she lightly touched my arm.

Now it was my turn to laugh. "Yep, *that* is an understatement!" I said, remembering the Doc saying the same thing to me more than once. Jane was not laughing anymore. I thought it was funny, but apparently Jane did not.

"We need to change that," she said. "Let's start with your name."

"What about my name?" I asked, sitting back a little and trying to put some distance between us.

"Well, the name Cathy is a bit boring," she said.

"And Jane isn't?" I piped back defensively.

"Yes, yes, Jane *is* a boring name, no doubt about that. But Cathy, do you think *I* am boring?"

"Jane, you are *hardly* boring. In fact, I wish I could be more like you. You are always smiling and sociable. I don't think you could *ever* be unhappy."

"What if you had a nickname, like Kat with a K. What do you think?" Jane said proudly.

I looked at Jane, wondering what was going on in that mind of hers. Kat with a K – I have to admit I *did* like it.

"Kat, Kat, Kat," Jane said. It seemed as though she was rehearsing for a play as she repeated my nickname a few times.

"Jane, the nickname is cute, but I'm not a Kardashian. Kat with a K sounds like I'm one of their long-lost daughters," I said, with some amusement. Now that was a funny thought – and maybe the next installment of my blank page – the long-lost Kardashian daughter. Knowing what I look like would prove that if I *am* a long-lost Kardashian, I was definitely adopted.

Jane laughed at the thought. "See, I knew you were funny, Kat."

"So, are you going to start calling me Kat from now on?" I asked.

"You bet!" Jane said, beaming, making the dark pub a little less gloomy.

"Okay, Kat, let's start drinking and see if there are any cute guys in this place," she added with some authority, as she started looking around the pub.

"Okay, looking for cute guys – why not?" I asked myself, sitting back in my chair and watching Jane turn her head from one side of the large room to the other. The pub was getting busy, with guys crowding around the bar. There were now only a few empty tables available. I could barely make out what song was playing because of the endless drone that was now vibrating through the pub. I followed Jane's lead, wondering about the cute guy with the wavy hair and wire-framed glasses, and feeling somewhat relieved to know that it was not Professor H.

I sat back in my chair nursing my beer, while Jane continued to look around the pub, occasionally asking me what I thought of that guy over at the bar or that guy standing next to the pool table. I would glance in the direction she was pointing and shrug my shoulders. I could tell Jane was getting frustrated with me, since my response each time was a shoulder shrug followed by "not my type." Jane must be trying to find someone for me, since the game continued for another hour.

After a second round of drinks, Jane and I stopped looking at guys and started asking about each other's life, with Jane sharing more of her past than I was ready to share of mine. I discovered that Jane's dad owned a popular furniture company in town. I'd never heard of the furniture store, but apparently it had been around for a while since Jane's family had owned it for at least two generations. Both Jane and her mom helped with the store's office work whenever someone called in sick or when her dad was trying to meet a deadline. I could feel the love Jane had for her parents each time she shared a funny tidbit about them. A twinge of jealousy crept into me while I hung on Jane's every word.

I was finishing my second light beer, when my mind started to get foggy.

"Jane, I think I should go home. I'm tired, and I have to work tomorrow," I said.

"Well okay, if you say so," Jane said, with a hint of disappointment.

I'd just pushed myself up from the hard chair and reached for my purse when Jane jumped up to give me a hug. I was startled and confused, since we had only just become friends. Isn't this a little early for hugging, I thought? I gave her my usual one-armed hug and thanked her for the fun.

I left a little disappointed that I never did see the cute guy with brown, wavy hair and wire-framed glasses, but at least I did get a nickname.

"Kat, Kat, Kat," I sang in a soft voice, strolling back to my car, laughing with a huge smile on my face – because I was beginning to sound like Jane.

I was happy to be home, even though I'd had fun with Jane. The more time I spent with her the more at ease I felt. Maybe she was right about a person coming into your life just at the right time, just when you needed them the most, but not really realizing it at the time.

I went to the kitchen after putting my jean jacket away. Fall was in the air and I felt chilled. Even though I loved my jean jacket, I knew I'd have to start wearing something heavier very soon. I made a cup of hot tea and sat down at the kitchen table, still chanting "Kat, Kat, Kat" in a sing-song voice. I wrapped my hands around the red cup, welcoming the smell of peppermint, and took a sip. The warm liquid seeped into my chilled body. I gently placed the cup on the kitchen table and pulled the top page off the stack of paper, placing it in front of me. Once again, the blank page was staring back at me, willing me to write.

With my eyes closed, I sat back and asked my question – Who am I? I remembered the evening at the pub with Jane. I remembered her giving me a new nickname – Kat. I thought of Kat. Kat would be more daring than Boring Cathy. If the cute guy with the dark, wavy hair and wire-framed glasses had entered the pub, Kat would have had said "hi" to him. Cathy would have just sat there, watching him out of the corner of her eye.

My eyes flew open and my hand instantly filled the blank page with words. Feelings were pouring out of me like water from a fountain. My hand flew across the page as I wrote about Kat having the courage to talk to a cute guy named Jeff. Kat and Jeff chatted. Jeff brought Kat a drink. They felt at ease with each other, almost as if they were meant to be together. Jeff kissed Kat, making her world blossom into a kaleidoscope of colors. Kat and Jeff fell in love. It was a simple and happy story. It was a fairy tale with Jeff becoming Kat's Prince Charming.

Chapter Eleven

It was the weekend, and I had to work the Saturday shift at the pillow factory. Saturdays were always lonely, since Fred refused to work on weekends. I wish I had that luxury. It was a quiet day, and I was able to get all the pillow orders packaged and ready for shipping before my shift was done. I spent what time was left cleaning the breakroom. My cell phone that was stuck in the back pocket of my work overalls rang, causing me to jump. I pulled the phone out of the pocket, wondering who could possibly be calling me and hoping that it wasn't the Doc. It was Jane.

"Hi Jane, what's up?" I asked.

"Hey Kat, what are you doing?" I could hear music in the background and wondered if Jane was still at the pub. She was right – I am silly.

"Oh I'm just finishing up my shift at work," I said.

"Where do you work?" she asked.

I'm certain Jane was not interested in where I worked or what I did. She was just being polite. I quickly explained about my boring job at the plant. I was right. She was being polite, since it felt as if I was talking to myself. I was okay with that, though, since it was nice to talk after a day filled with silence.

"Are you doing anything tonight?" she asked, after I gave her the limited highlights of my boring job.

What was I doing tonight? That was easy – nothing. I was looking forward to spending another night writing, which seemed strange, considering what Professor H had said to me a few weeks ago.

"Nothing, really. What do you have in mind?" I asked.

"I thought we could go to a nightclub. A new club opened a few weeks ago. From what I've heard, it's the hottest place in town," Jane said, in a very excited voice.

The thought of going to a nightclub sent chills up and down my spine. I've never been to one, and I definitely didn't have anything to wear. What would I do once I got there, I thought? The excuses for not going bombarded my brain.

"Jane I don't think I can make it. I don't have anything to wear. My wardrobe is not nightclub worthy," I said, slightly embarrassed and slightly relieved.

"Oh, Kat," Jane laughed. "I'm positive I can find something in my closet for you to wear. I'm certain we're the same size. Just come to my house when you get off work."

I had to think that once again Jane was drinking something. I'm not the same size as she is. I was about to decline, when I heard the voices – *my* voice – asking "Who am I?" and another voice telling me I needed to break out of my self-created shell. Going to the nightclub might help me find out who I could be. It would definitely push me beyond my comfort zone. I also got the feeling that I would never be able to win an argument against Jane.

"Okay, Jane," I said with a heavy sigh. "I'll go." I wondered if she could hear the fear in my voice.

I found a scrap of paper and wrote down Jane's address. I told her that I would be at her house in about an hour.

It was fairly easy to find Jane's neighborhood. One big house after another had been strategically placed to form a circular pattern. Each one had its house number in front, on a wide, flat rock, in large and elaborate numbers. It was almost as if the rock served as a beacon, saying to all who passed by, "Look at me, look at me!" I was in awe as I slowly drove by each house, trying to find Jane's. Each house had a huge and gorgeous front yard, with everything perfectly painted in place. The trees were displaying their colorful splendor of vibrant red and orange leaves. I stopped my car in front of Jane's house, thinking perfect house, perfect yard, and perfect family. Jane was lucky.

The outside light was on, illuminating my way up a cobblestone path that led to the front porch. A gentle breeze whispered past me. I looked up and saw the sliver of a moon, and the first star, peeking through a rosy sky. I smiled, returning my attention to Jane's house and the cobblestone path ahead of me. I walked up the path, stopping in front of a gorgeous red door that served as the gateway to Jane's home. I had never seen a red door before. Who has a front door that was red, I thought? Well, Jane of course.

I pushed the doorbell alongside the red door. I scanned the front porch, tapping one foot and waiting for someone to answer the door. There were two white rocking chairs on the left side of a porch, which seemed to wrap continuously around the entire house. I was reaching for the doorbell when I heard footsteps rushing towards the door with a tap, tap, tap. I rubbed my hands together to stop the nervousness that was coursing through me. Who was going to be opening the door – her dad, her mom, or maybe a butler? If anyone had a butler, it would be Jane.

The gorgeous red door flew open, with Jane standing breathless in the doorway. "Kat!" she screamed, with more enthusiasm than I had ever witnessed. Who knew my presence could cause someone to be so happy? I wish I were the type of person who could jump up and down, but I was not. I could not join Jane in her happy dance. I did give her my usual one-arm hug as I said hello.

She grabbed my hands, pulling me into a big entryway. I looked up to the ceiling, thinking that the entryway was as big as, if not bigger than, my little apartment. Brightness surrounded me, with a huge chandelier hanging from the ceiling and a shiny white marble floor beneath my feet.

Being in Jane's enormous home brought back thoughts of my little home with Mom. It was simple and small, but comfortable. I was lucky to have my own bathroom and bedroom. Jane's home must have numerous bedrooms and bathrooms, I thought.

"Wow, Jane, your home is amazing. Is it all yours?" I asked, still scanning the entryway, my eyes wide with wonder.

"Oh, silly Kat, of course not. This is my parents' house," she said. "Now follow me; we don't have a lot of time."

Jane turned and I obediently followed her up a white staircase that curved up to the second floor. The cream-colored carpet was thick, as each step I took barely made a sound. Family photos were strategically placed along the wall of the staircase. Most of the photos were of a young girl with blonde hair at various ages. The girl had to have been Jane. The hallway formed a T when we got to the top of the long staircase, with Jane's bedroom at one end of the T and her parents' room at the other end. My mouth dropped when we entered her huge bedroom. It was just as bright as the entryway, with white and various shades of pink splashed throughout the room. Jane walked over to one side of her bedroom and opened two large doors. A light automatically came on. The doors led to a walk-in closet that was jammed with clothes, shoes, and purses. Jane disappeared into the closet and then emerged, carrying a colorful armload of dresses. I watched her walk over to the bed, dropping the dresses onto the bed, and prayed that at least one of them would fit me.

I stared at the pile of clothes on Jane's gorgeous four-poster bed, wondering where to start. The fluffy white bedspread buried beneath the pile reminded me of a puffy cloud. Big white pillows trimmed with pink ribbon were strategically placed at the top of the bed. There was a white desk with a pink laptop and a framed photo on top of the desk. Maybe, I thought, I could ask Jane about buying a laptop.

I picked up the first thing that drew my attention – a blue dress that had long sleeves and a bit of silver in the top. The fabric felt extremely soft. I thought about how comforting it would be to wrap the dress around me and take a nap, rather than getting dressed up for the nightclub. I went into Jane's bathroom, which was just off her bedroom. Jane's bathroom was just as bright and pink as her bedroom. I got the impression that Jane's favorite color was pink. It took me a while to figure out how to put on the pretty blue dress. The sleeves were strange, and there was a sash that wrapped around my body, but I could not figure how that worked. Jane was yelling for me to hurry up, and how the nightclub would close before we get there.

"Jane," I called out. "I think I need to try on a different dress. I look like a blue elephant in this one."

Jane threw two more dresses into the bathroom. I'm glad Jane suspected that I was a little shy. One of the two was a very short red dress. It was super cute and very sexy, something I would see in a Cosmo ad. "Do I dare try on such a dress" I asked myself? The red dress was a lot easier to get into than the blue one. I was shocked to discover that the dress *did* fit. Jane was right. I *didn't* need to lose weight, and we *were* about the same size. I was even more shocked to see that I looked good in the dress. I mean *really* good. I went closer to the full-length mirror to study myself. I looked into my eyes and whispered, "Who are you?" I looked deeper into my eyes, and then at myself in the red dress. I can be a girl who was going out to a nightclub, I thought.

"Oh Kat...? Remember me – the girlfriend who is taking you out to the nightclub? We need to go soon."

Jane's somewhat impatient voice broke my happy dream. I left the security of Jane's bathroom, feeling a little self-conscious. I do believe Jane was more shocked than I was to see me in that dress, since for once I saw Jane's mouth drop open.

"Well, what do you think?" I hesitantly asked, looking off to the side instead of directly at Jane.

"Wow, Kat, you are better looking than I thought you would be," Jane said, somewhat in disbelief.

"Gee thanks, Jane. I'll take that as a compliment."

"Well, it was. Now you need some shoes and makeup, and then we can go," Jane said, this time with the usual "let's get down to business" tone in her voice.

Shoes I can handle, I thought. Makeup – well, that was another story. I always thought it would be fun to go to a makeup counter at one of the big department stores to get a makeover. The ladies at work would talk about getting a makeover, especially when they had a hot date. Even though I toyed with the idea of getting one myself, I never did. What good would it do, since I never had a hot date? And besides, what would I look like afterwards – not to mention that I could never replicate what they did to me. And so it never happened.

"Hmm, Jane, I've never worn makeup before," I quietly said, looking down at the floor and feeling embarrassed.

"Oh, Kat, tell me something I didn't already know. I'll put just a bit of makeup on you myself. Don't worry – I'm a pro," Jane said.

In minutes, Jane quickly applied eye shadow, eyeliner, and mascara to my virgin face. I admired the face that was gazing back at me, thinking that Jane was right, she *was* a pro.

"Okay, now we have to find you some shoes, since sneakers won't work," Jane said.

Jane's feet were slightly bigger than mine, which shocked me. She seemed so petite. Don't petite women have petite feet? Jane was able to find a pair of shoes that did fit me. They were her mother's. Thank goodness the heels were not as high as Jane's. The shoes were silver, which was exactly what Jane wanted for me.

I felt like Jane's life-size Barbie. I had to suppress my laughter at the irony. I don't think I could ever be honest enough to tell Jane that I thought she looked like a Barbie the first time I saw her. Jane added some finishing touches – earrings and a handbag – before swinging me around to face the mirror.

My jaw dropped. That *can't* be me, I thought. I barely recognized the girl that was staring back at me. I stepped a little closer to the mirror, turning my head one way and then the other. I turned around in a slow circle, watching myself move in the mirror, a flash of red trailing me. I felt as if I were a blank piece of paper, onto which Jane had painted a picture of beautiful girl. I looked amazing, if I could say that about myself. A flood of emotions that I had suppressed for some time came rushing back.

I had been getting ready for a homecoming dance. It was one of the few times that I had gone to a dance at all, and one of the few times a boy had asked me to a dance. Mom found me a formal dress at a local thrift store for the event. The dress was a simple, white, floor-length grown with a princess neck. Mom was amazing with a needle and thread, and she added a few unique touches such as a rhinestone trim around the waist and down the sleeves. The dress flowed like a wisp of cloud when I moved. I twirled in a circle as Mom studied her final touches. I looked like an angel, even with my straight hair and no make-up. I smiled as I remembered twirling in a circle, watching the dress slightly billow around me, and seeing a glimpse of a smile from Mom as she watched. I remember Mom having the same pleased expression on her face then that Jane had now. I turned away so that Jane would not see the tears that were threatening. I pushed back the thought and the tears so that I would not ruin my makeup.

I took another look at the new me that was standing in the mirror and whispered "Who am I, Mom?" I wished Mom was here to give me an answer, and to see me now.

Chapter Twelve

There was a line out the door when we finally made it to the nightclub. Jane was right; it was a popular place. Disappointment rushed through me when I saw the long line.

"Oh, Jane, I'm so sorry. I don't think we're ever going to get in. It's my fault for taking so long to get ready," I said, with regret in my voice. I wanted to add that I was afraid I was not going to be able to stand in these shoes much longer, but I bit my lip before spewing out those words.

"Kat, don't worry – I have a plan. You stay here, and I'll be right back." Jane muttered the words before leaving me and headed towards the entrance. I could sense a bit of frustration from her, which made me feel even worse. I was really surprised that she hadn't made some comment, like "If only you hadn't taken so long." But she didn't. I had to think that Jane was a good friend and a good person. I never would have guessed that when I first saw her.

I waited in line for about five minutes, even though it felt like thirty as far as my feet were concerned. More and more people arrived, making the line grow behind me. Just when I was questioning my earlier thoughts of Jane being a good person, and now thinking that she'd taken off without me, Jane came back with her high heels, making a quick tap, tap, tap sound. I was in awe at how quickly she could walk in those stilts.

"Kat, follow me," Jane said, grabbing my hand and pulling me out of the line.

"Jane, are we leaving?" I asked. "I'm really sorry that I took so long to get ready. I know that if it wasn't for me we would already be inside," I said, feeling defeated and ashamed.

"Oh, don't be silly, Kat." Jane laughed as she continued to pull me towards the front door of the club. "I have connections at the front door. My father is really good friends with the father of the security guy who is working the entrance. I haven't seen Paul in ages. That's his name. I had to see if he could sneak us in. Of course I had to catch up with him. That was why it took me so long to get back to you. I'm just glad that Paul doesn't find me interesting. Just so you know, I was ready to promise a date with him just to get us inside. You do know you owe me, right?" I was amazed that Jane was able to say all that while quickly walking in the stilts and not taking a single breath. I was gasping for air just trying to keep up with her.

Jane wrapped one arm around me and pushed me through the front door of the most popular nightclub in town. A rush of music and heat greeted us. I whispered to myself, "Who am I now?" as I turned around to see lights flashing throughout the gigantic room. "I am a girl in a nightclub – that's who I am," I said to myself. I was giddy as I repeated those words inside my head and slowly turned in a circle, taking in all the action that surrounded me.

The nightclub was packed, with a sea of bodies trying to move among and against each other. Some were going to the bar, others were trying to find a space on the dance floor, and even more of them were standing against a wall or table, checking out the scene and seeing the latest girl or boy who had just entered. Tiny lights sparkled around the room, and the music blared. I could feel the bass of the music vibrating through my body. Now *this* was bold, I said to myself.

I followed Jane's lead as we made the mandatory stroll around the club before getting a drink and finding a spot to stand. Free chairs did not exist, which sent up a groan from my feet. We gracefully propped ourselves against one of the many pillars that were scattered throughout the nightclub, and watched the people dancing and the latest group entering the room. Jane would occasionally point to a guy, asking me what I thought of him. Yes, she was still trying to set me up. I would just shake my head from side to side. I was still trying to find that cute guy with the dark, wavy hair and wire-framed glasses. Jane was chatting with Paul, who was on break, and I continued to scan the crowd, when my heart skipped a beat. I could see the outline of a tall guy over near the bar who seemed to have wavy hair. I squinted, trying to get a better look, when the tall figure turned to face in my general direction. He too was scanning the nightclub, with a drink in his hand. I had to wonder who he was looking for. I noticed that the tall guy had wire-framed glasses as the lights from the numerous disco balls danced off his glasses. And then my mouth dropped. It was Professor H.

I nudged Jane just at the same time she was saying good-bye to Paul. Jane turned her attention to me, and I discreetly pointed in his direction, hoping that Professor H did not notice me staring and pointing at him. Just at that moment Professor H noticed us, or at least he noticed Jane. He too seemed surprised, but handled it better than I had as he raised his glass in our direction in a gesture to say "hi."

"Jane, do you think he recognizes me" I asked. I could feel the fear developing in the pit of my stomach as bees began to hum. I don't know why I should be afraid of him. We weren't in the classroom.

Jane laughed. "Kat. I'm certain he doesn't realize who you are. He may recognize me, or at least I hope he does. I'm going to say hi to him. Did you want to join me?"

My throat went dry and the Cathy – also known as the coward – reappeared, taking over Kat's body.

"Nope, I think I'll stay right here. You have a crush on him. I just think he's good looking. You should go by yourself. And please don't tell him I'm here. Just pretend that I'm *not* here." I could tell that my voice was quivering. Jane looked at me, wondering if something was wrong, but just shrugged her shoulders.

"Okay, well, don't say I didn't give you a chance," Jane said, patting her dress down and fluffing her gorgeous blonde hair up a bit. "How do I look?"

"Gorgeous as always, Jane," I said, with a hint of pride in my voice.

Jane smiled, placing her glass on a nearby shelf, and sauntered over to Professor H. I watched as Jane carefully, and with very little effort, made her way through the crowd. I was in awe, watching her glide through the crowd, since I would have tripped over my feet.

I saw the entire act play out in front of me. Jane introduced herself to Professor H. You could tell that he knew who she was. There was a brief exchange of words. I saw Professor H glance in my direction, while nodding his head and listening to Jane. I quickly looked away, acting if I were scanning the crowd. I took the chance to glance back at Jane and Professor H to see Jane pointing to the dance floor. Professor H shrugged his shoulders, maybe in defeat, since how can you refuse Jane? Perhaps there was a human beneath his tough exterior after all,

I thought. Professor H placed his drink down on the bar and followed Jane to the dance floor.

He must feel okay about dancing with one of his students, I thought. I smiled, happy for Jane. I took turns scanning the huge nightclub and watching Professor H and Jane dance. My feet were starting to ache as I shifted my weight from one foot to the other, hoping that would help. I was definitely getting tired of standing. I looked around the room trying to find someone I knew, but that was unlikely. My coworkers at the plant wouldn't be caught dead in a nightclub. The scene was definitely too young for them. Also, they seem to prefer the pub-and-jeans atmosphere to this sort of glitz. I have to admit that at this point I too would prefer being at the pub right now, wearing sneakers, instead of these stilts that are making my feet throb.

I turned to find the ladies room, thinking that I could sit on the counter or the toilet to help alleviate the throbbing in my feet, when I saw him – the tall, good-looking guy from my business class. Instead of my mouth dropping the way it did when I saw Professor H, or my breath getting caught in my throat the way it did when I first saw the cute guy, I got excited. The "what ifs" started spinning in my head. I forgot about looking for the ladies room as I watched him and his buddies. Rather than scanning the nightclub like every other guy, they were crouched together, as if they were having a very important conversation about saving the world. I stood as still as I possible and watched him. I thought about walking over to his table, but I knew deep down inside that I would not. Why isn't Jane here, I thought. She would know what to do. I looked out onto the dance floor, hoping to see Jane, but I couldn't find her in the moving sea of people. Great, I thought. *Now* what should I do?

I looked back at the group of guys, and decided to be part of the numerous shadows that were flickering in the nightclub, when the tall, cute guy looked up in my direction. Once again our eyes locked. Instead of my heart stopping, my stomach started fluttering. It was a mixture of excitement and apprehension. And just as he had in class, he smiled. I smiled back, feeling hopeful. Could he really like me? Does he even recognize me? The questions bombarded my mind as I thought about what to do next. The tall, good-looking guy released our visual connection and bent over to say something to the guy sitting next to him. My heart sank. He was just being nice I thought. Feeling defeated, I turned to go find the bathroom since my feet had resumed their chant. I'd taken a few steps towards the hallway when I felt something warm and strong touching my shoulder. I should have been startled by the touch, but I wasn't. I turned to see the tall, cute guy looking down at me, his hand on my bare shoulder. His steel-blue eyes were hypnotizing. "Keep your mouth closed," I said to myself, "and breathe."

"Hi. You look familiar. Have we met?" he asked, in a deep yet soothing voice.

I don't know what caused me to lose my voice more, his eyes or his voice. I guess he didn't recognize me. I had to wonder if I should tell him that we have a business class together or let him figure it out. I swallowed. He was even better looking close up. He had a strong nose that was not big, but fit his face perfectly. A hint of dark stubble was just appearing along his chin and jawbone. And of course there was the brown, wavy hair that hung just past his ears. I noticed a small rhinestone earring in his right ear that winked back at me. He was wearing the same jean jacket he'd worn in class with a black T-shirt underneath. I was a little surprised that he was dressed so casually. The other guys at the nightclub were wearing polo shirts or crisp, collared shirts with their jeans or khakis. Not the tall, good-looking guy. Maybe he wasn't here to impress anyone or to pick up a girl. Maybe he was just here to hang out with his friends. I could tell that he was wondering if I'd heard his question, since he removed his hand from my shoulder and shoved it in the pocket of his jeans, maybe thinking he'd made a mistake and wasn't certain what to do next. I could still feel the heat of his touch on my shoulder.

"We have business class together," I said in a low voice, hoping that he could not hear the nervousness that was swirling in my belly and attaching itself to my words. I was kicking myself for not saying more, but not really knowing what more I should say. The tall, good-looking guy bent down, getting a little closer, when a wave of recognition appeared in the form of another smile, along with a twinkle in his steel-blue eyes. This smile was just as infectious as the one he'd given me on the first day of class. I sucked in a deep breath, smelling the hint of something clean, like Ivory soap.

"Of course," he said, still smiling. "You look a little different. Maybe it's because of the lights here, or really in this case, the lack thereof," he added, with a little laugh. "You were sitting alone in the back of the classroom?"

He does remember me. I absorbed each word leaving his lips with the word "alone" vibrating in my head. Yes, I was alone, I thought. I was sitting alone in the back of the classroom, because that's where I feel the safest. I didn't know what to say after that.

"Are you here alone?" he added, and backed away, looking around to see if anyone was coming towards us, towards me.

At least I was not alone at the nightclub. If the tall, good-looking guy knew me, he would know that I would never venture into a nightclub – or really anywhere else – alone.

"No, I'm here with my girlfriend. She's dancing with someone right now." I tried to sound upbeat, but I was feeling lost. I had to wonder what he thought of me now. Maybe he was feeling sorry for me, because he thought I'm always alone. I did notice that he stopped scanning the room, and returned his attention to me.

"My name is Ryan," he said, with his hands still in his pockets. "Would you like to sit with me and my friends while you wait for your girlfriend? It might be nice to sit rather than stand. I don't know how you can stand wearing those shoes. Don't get me wrong – they look great, especially on you – but..." And then he chuckled as he looked down at the silver spikes I was wearing. Relief flooded my body as I thought about finally sitting down. I had to wonder if the tall, good-looking guy was a mind reader. I wanted to give him a big hug but decided I'd better not. I would definitely scare him if I did, and I am not a big hugger like Jane.

"Ryan, my feet would love to sit down," I said with a smile. I was amazed at how easy it was to smile around him. "My name is Ca..., Kat," I said, thinking Jane would have been proud of me for using my nickname.

"It's nice to finally meet you, Kat. That's a pretty cool name. Follow me, and we'll give your feet a much-needed break," Ryan beamed, before turning and walking towards his friends.

I followed as best I could. I had to take four shuffles to his two steps, which was challenging in heels. I kept my gaze on his back, walking as gracefully as I could and praying that I would not trip. I kept thinking of Jane and how effortlessly she'd floated towards Professor H. I imagined clouds as I tried to do the same. I successfully floated to the table, giving myself a mental pat on the back before releasing the breath that I had been holding. Ryan introduced me to his friends, Austin, Nick, and Justin. The three guys said hi before moving closer together, freeing up two chairs. I sat down, feeling happy that I was sitting, but also feeling self-conscious sitting with a bunch of guys. Ryan sat down too, moving his chair a little closer to mine so that our chairs formed a V. The three guys resumed their important conversation. Ryan and I sat, looking out to the dance floor, with our backs to his three friends. I felt a little rude with my back to them, but they didn't seem to mind and neither did Ryan. The silence between us grew awkward. I tried to think of what to say. Where was Jane when I needed her, I thought? I was beginning to wonder if Jane had run off with Professor H and was living her wildest dream when Ryan broke the silence. I was so caught up in my own thoughts that I didn't hear what he'd said. Great, he will definitely think I'm rude. I moved closer to Ryan so I would not miss another word. The bass of the music was still causing the room to vibrate, making it hard to hear. I had to wonder if the vibrating was from the music or my nerves. I mean, seriously – Ryan, the tall, good-looking guy with the brown, wavy hair was talking to me.

"I'm sorry, Ryan, I didn't hear you. I was lost in the wonderful feeling of not standing."

Ryan laughed as he bent over, letting his forearms rest on his thighs and bringing his head closer to mine. I took a deep breath, letting the fresh scent of soap calm my senses. It was then that I noticed his knee was touching my thigh. An urge to move my leg automatically kicked in, but I decided to ignore it.

"I just asked if you have been to this nightclub before. I've never seen you here before."

"This is my first time. My friend Jane wanted to try it out, since she had heard a lot about it. It seems like a popular place." I glanced behind me to see if his friends were still engrossed in their conversation or if they'd decided to eavesdrop. They were still oblivious to us.

"Don't worry about them. They're talking about the tournament we have tomorrow. They didn't want to leave the house, but I convinced them that it would be a good distraction."

"Tournament – what type of tournament?" I was intrigued and a little surprised. I didn't think *I* would be going out if I had something important the next day.

"It's a softball tournament. It isn't a big deal. At least I don't think so. I just like to play and have fun. Justin takes the game very seriously." Ryan gave another chuckle as he tilted his head in the direction of his friends, probably in the direction of Justin. "Have you ever played softball?"

Now it was my turn to laugh. I'd never played sports. Mom didn't encourage it, so I didn't see the need to try out for any sports. I do remember having fun playing basketball and running track, in physical education, when I was in high school. I had to wonder if I could even run a block right now. I knew I couldn't in these shoes.

"No, I've never played softball, or really any sport." I felt myself moving closer and closer to Ryan. The nervousness I'd once been feeling faded away. I was amazed at how easy it was to talk to him, almost as if we were old friends. I definitely liked it when he laughed.

There was another long pause. I had to wonder if he'd heard me, since another song was booming in the background. I looked to see that Ryan was no longer smiling, but seemed a little puzzled, almost as if he was thinking of something important. I saw his Adam's apple move up and down as he swallowed.

"Would you like to go to the tournament tomorrow?" I could feel the excitement in his voice when he asked me. I could also feel the nervousness creeping back in, and I started to fidget in my chair. How could I possibly go to a tournament with a guy I just met? Who would do that? Well, Jane would, but not boring Cathy. And then I remembered that I was Kat – and *not* boring Cathy! My squirming caused me to move my leg away from Ryan's knee, and he noticed. He also noticed that I'd become very quiet. If only he knew that the silence between us was because of the constant chattering in my mind, my own personal battle raging on.

"Hey Kat, it's okay if you aren't interested," he said, with a hint of disappointment.

Why was he being so nice to me, I thought? I can barely wrap my head around having Jane like me – and now Ryan. It would be fun to watch the game, but I wouldn't know anyone, and I have to work tomorrow. I stopped fidgeting and moved my thigh so that it was touching Ryan's knee. I could hear Ryan let out a long breath. Almost as if he was the one holding his breath this time.

"Ryan, I think it would be fun to go, but I have to work tomorrow," I said, looking at him but avoiding his eyes. I would definitely skip work if I got lost in his eyes, I thought, and I could not do that. I did see relief wash across Ryan's face as the muscles in his jaw relaxed.

"Oh, not a problem," Ryan said, pushing himself back a little in his chair without moving his knee. "I definitely understand having to work. Maybe you can make it to the next tournament." I could tell he turned to look at me as he said this, with a sly grin crossing his face. Butterflies were fluttering in my stomach, making my body feel light and happy. I looked out onto the dance floor, enjoying the feeling and not minding the silence.

"Would you like to dance, if your feet are okay with it?" Ryan said, with a touch of humor in his voice.

This time I laughed. "My feet would love to dance – at least I think they would," I said, shifting my attention from the dance floor to Ryan.

Ryan pushed himself up from his chair, taking my hand and then guiding me to the dance floor. I was a little shocked and giddy by his forwardness. He really was the nicest guy I'd ever met.

Ryan and I did our best to move our feet to the music without crashing into each other, or bumping into someone else. There were times when a guy or girl who was getting into the song would collide with us, causing us to bump into each other. Each time, Ryan and I would either smile or laugh. And each time I would smell the hint of a clean breeze. I had to wonder what his cologne was, because I liked it. It reminded me of clouds floating in the sky after a gentle spring rain.

Ryan and I danced a few more songs, our bodies getting closer and closer with each one. There was a break in the music, and I thought that this would be my chance to ask Ryan if we could sit down. I couldn't ignore the throbbing in my feet. Ryan turned to me, his strong hands reaching for mine. Warmth in the center of my belly radiated throughout my body. We stood facing each other, almost as if we were both afraid to move. Ryan was looking down at me and I was looking up at him. I forgot about my aching feet. I forgot about the crowd surrounding us. I was lost in the depths of blue skies that swirled around me. It was just Ryan and me on the dance floor. And then someone bumped into me, pulling me back to reality.

We were not alone. I let out a sigh, and pulled myself out of the cloud I was floating in.

"Ryan, I need to go find my friend," I whispered, not really wanting to leave him but knowing that I had to. "Thank you for the dance."

Ryan's hands were still gently wrapped around mine as he moved his gaze from my eyes to the top of my head. I closed my eyes, feeling the heat from his gaze and the heat from his touch. Ryan released one of my hands and smiled.

"Yeah, I probably need to get the guys back to the house so they don't sleep during tomorrow's game," Ryan said. He turned and walked me off the dance floor and towards the table where his buddies were still sitting. I guess they had solved the mysteries of the world, or tomorrow's tournament, since they were no longer huddled together but sitting back in their chairs, looking out into the crowd. One of them, I can't remember his name, saw Ryan and waved him over, giving the impression that he was ready to leave. Ryan waved back.

"I've got to go. I can tell Justin has had enough," Ryan said, turning his gaze down at me and placing one hand on my shoulder. His touch was warm and reassuring. I was speechless. I did not know how to say good-bye. Should I ask for his number? Why isn't he asking for *my* number? Should I say "see you later"? Instead of saying anything, I turned and walked away from Ryan.

I walked back to the bar, looking for Jane, when I decided to glance over my shoulder to take a final look at Ryan. My heart fluttered when I saw that Ryan was looking back at me. This time I was the one who smiled first, causing Ryan to smile and wave. I waved back, with my smile getting bigger and my body feeling lighter. I was just wishing that the lightness I was feeling would transfer to my feet, but it didn't.

I turned back, making my way to the crowded area where Jane and I had started, only to find a new group of girls and guys standing in our spot. Jane was not there. I did the walk around the club, even though my feet were screaming for me not to take another step. I didn't see Jane anywhere, so I decided to check the ladies' restroom. At least I would be able to sit down there, and give my feet a much-needed break.

I sat on the toilet longer than I needed to, but it felt so good to sit. I was not looking forward to standing and walking in those shoes anytime soon. I wondered what people would think if I'd walked out barefoot, twirling the silver stilts in one hand. I could hear a line forming outside the stall, with an occasional tapping of a shoe on the tile floor. I took a deep breath, willing my feet to hold on just a little longer, as I got up and left the ladies' room to search for Jane once more.

After taking another lap around the nightclub I finally saw Jane dancing, but not with Professor H. I waved, trying to catch her attention, as she bobbed to the beat of the music. She waved back, letting me know that she'd seen me. I rested against an available spot on the wall and waited for the song to end. I turned to the table where Ryan and his buddies had been sitting, only to see that they had left. I was relieved when I saw Jane leave the dance floor and start walking towards me.

"Hey Kat, isn't this place great?" Jane said, with more enthusiasm than a normal person would express.

I was feeling a little guilty wanting to leave, but I was so tired and my feet could not take any more standing. "Jane, I hate to ask, but can we please go home?" I'm certain it sounded more like a plea then a question.

"Aren't you having fun?" she asked. "I saw you dancing with some guy."

"It's not that, it just that my feet are killing me," I whined.

"Oh, I got it; you're not used to the shoes. I can relate. My feet are starting to hurt too. It's a shame, though, because Professor H was asking who you were," Jane said, bumping my shoulder with a quick wink.

I hoped Jane was the only one who saw my mouth drop.

"Kat, you need to close your mouth. You look silly," Jane said.

I closed my mouth after taking a big gulp of air. "What did he what to know? What did you tell him?" Both sentences came out almost at the same time.

"Don't worry. He just knows that you are Kat, and a good friend of mine. He did want to meet you, but fortunately for me, you disappeared." Jane gave me a funny smile, and I wasn't certain of its meaning. I was relieved that I hadn't been around to meet Professor H.

"Where have you been? I've been looking for you for at least an hour. One minute I saw you dancing with a cute guy, and the next minute you were gone. So who was he, and does he have any friends?" she asked, with too much humor in her voice.

"After dancing with him, I went to the only place I knew where I could sit down, the bathroom."

"That was very clever. But who's the guy, and does he have any friends?"

"His name is Ryan, he's in my business class, and yes he has friends, but I don't think they would be your type unless you like softball."

"Softball?" Jane asked, raising one eyebrow. I'm glad to know that I was not the only one unfamiliar with softball.

"Yes, Ryan invited me to watch a softball tournament tomorrow. He and his friends are on the team."

"Well, look at you, Miss Kat. I can't say that I would be interested in watching a softball tournament, but I am proud of you," Jane said, wrapping her arm around me and pulling me away from the wall that was supporting me and relieving some of the pressure from my feet. I was feeling proud of myself, too, as I let Jane squeeze me. "I'm ready to go when you are. Professor H has left, and I'm not interested in anyone else here."

"Did Professor H ask for your number?" I asked, trying to change the topic.

"No, he didn't." Jane's shoulders sank slightly, causing her to look as though she had just lost a battle. "And besides, it would not be right to date him since I'm taking his class. Now I'm asking myself why I took his class in the first place. Oh Kat, sometimes you just can't win," Jane said with a slight huff.

"Jane," I thought to myself, "I have been asking myself that question ever since that Assignment from Hell."

Chapter Thirteen

It was the middle of the semester – meaning another week of classes, and another creative writing class with the ever-so-cute and ever-so-abrasive Professor H. More importantly, it also meant another exciting business class and the chance to see Ryan. I pushed the covers to the side and jumped out of bed, relieved that I hadn't had any nightmares that might have caused me to wake up late. Instead I had plenty of time to get ready, and I was excited.

I took a longer-than-usual shower, enjoying the warm water hitting my body and the steam billowing around me. The scent of citrus filled the air. I took a deep breath, letting the bright scent penetrate and awaken my senses. I thought of Ivory soap, and the hope of seeing Ryan this week brought another wave of happiness. Ryan hadn't been in class last week, which was disappointing and made for a longer-than-usual business class. I turned the water off and grabbed a thick towel.

The mirror still had a misty film even after I was dressed. Wow, I must have taken a really hot shower, I thought. I thought about wiping my hand across the mirror so that I could see myself and ask the question. I continued to stare at the mirror, seeing my blurry outline, and thinking about the question. I leaned on the bathroom sink, bringing myself closer to the mirror; minutes passed as the misty film slowly faded, allowing my features to become more defined. I could see my hazel eyes staring back at me with a touch of humor around them. I could see my long, brown hair still wet from my shower. My thin, pink lips were slightly curled up with the hint of a smile. I took a deep breath, the light scent of citrus still floating in the air. I pushed myself away from the bathroom sink and went to the kitchen to grab a cup of coffee.

I glanced at the kitchen table and the stack of blank paper that had once taunted me. I was pleased to see that the stack of paper was dwindling. I discovered that it was easier to write when you believed you were someone else, and this past weekend at the nightclub provided a lot of material as I covered several blank pages with word after word and line after line. The more I wrote, the easier it got. I was no longer intimidated by the whiteness of the blank page. In fact, I started to gaze at the page in admiration as I would gently tap my pen on my lip, thinking of what to write. I would close my eyes just for a moment, visualizing the thoughts that were spinning in my mind. Once I gathered those thoughts, I would open my eyes and let the pen fly across the page, as if my hand had a mind of its own.

It was the end of class and Professor H did not give us a homework assignment. I had to breathe a sigh of relief, even though I was starting to enjoy the class – or at least the writing portion of the class. I was excited that I had completed last week's homework assignment, and I could only hope that Professor H would be pleased too. I walked down the steps to the front of the classroom with my completed assignment in hand. My legs did not feel like lead and there were no bees buzzing in my stomach. I placed my homework on the top of the other completed assignments. Professor H was at his desk, his attention on something in front of him and not on the stack of completed assignments. I turned and started strolling out the door, thinking that maybe today I would make it to biology on time, when Professor H called my name. I stopped dead in my tracks, as an icy dread knotted in the pit of my stomach. *Now what had I done, or not done, I thought?*

I had always heard stories about how teachers or professors had it in for a particular student. You never really knew why they didn't like that student. Maybe it was because the student looked like someone the teacher didn't like, or maybe the student reminded them of an ex-boyfriend, husband, girlfriend, or wife. I was beginning to think that I was Professor H's problem student, and I wondered why he could not find me less memorable.

I slowly turned and walked back to his desk, feeling as though this was my death march.

"Yes, Professor Hanson?" I said, once I was next to his desk, hoping that he could not hear the fear in my voice. I looked down, not because I did not want him to recognize that I was Kat from the nightclub, but because I was afraid. I felt as if I was back in sixth grade, and I was being kept after school because of something I had done.

"I finally had a chance to read the assignment you turned in a couple of weeks ago. You know, the one to make up for the assignment we had on the first day of class?" he said.

I shifted from one foot to the other, thinking about that first day of class. How could I forget!

"Yes, I remember," I said quietly. "Was it bad? Do you want me to drop the class?" The words were pouring out of my mouth. "Idiot, idiot, idiot," I repeated to myself.

Professor H chuckled, shattering my dark mood. I looked up to see if he was really laughing, because who thought the guy could laugh? Statues don't laugh. Could he possibly be human, I thought?

"No, Cathy – quite the opposite. I thought it was good. I'm not certain what happened to make you tap into your creative juices, but you did. Maybe you were just a little nervous, since it was the first day of the class," he said, in a slightly humorous tone.

Yes, maybe that was it, I thought, that and the fact that I don't know who I am. There was also the fact that Professor H was very good looking and could make any woman nervous. I had to wonder if he made Jane nervous. Hardly, I said to myself – Jane feeling nervous because of Professor H was definitely a silly thought. Maybe Jane was right – I *am* funny.

"What was that, Cathy?" Professor H asked, pulling me back to reality.

"Oh, nothing," I added. "I think you're right. I was really nervous the first day of class. It has been a while since I've been in school, and I was really questioning myself."

"Well, you can stop questioning yourself. You're doing better. And I am glad to know that you are here for the right reasons. I look forward to reading your next assignment," Professor Hanson added, as he returned his attention to his desk.

"Okay, Professor H. Can I leave now? I don't want to be late for my next class," I asked, trying to suppress my excitement. Then I was thinking, did I really need to ask for his permission to leave? Why does he make me feel like I'm back in high school?

"Yes, Cathy, you can leave," he said, with a little chuckle.

There it was again – that laugh. I must admit I kind of like the laugh, I thought, as I turned and quickly walked out of the classroom before he'd had a chance to think of something else to say. The laugh made him seem more human and less abrasive.

As soon as I got past the doorway, I turned to start running down the hallway – and I collided with Jane, who was once again waiting for me outside the classroom. "Wow, Jane," I said, coming to an abrupt halt.

"Okay, Kat, if I didn't know better I would say that Professor H has a crush on you and you feel the same way. Now spill it, tell me the truth." I could hear Jane tapping her shoe.

I was shocked by Jane's accusation.

"Listen, Jane, you are my friend and I know that you have the hots for him. Anyway, he was just saying that my latest assignment was a big improvement from the first assignment. That was it. Jane, you have nothing to worry about." I placed my hand on her shoulder, hoping that this would reassure her.

"*Now* who's being the silly one," Jane said with a little giggle. Even with the giggle, I could still tell she was upset.

"Jane, you are never silly, and you have nothing to worry about. Now I have to run to biology before I'm late again." I gave Jane my one-arm hug before turning and running down the hallway.

Once again I was late for biology, and once again I had to sit in the front row. If any professor was going to ask me to drop a class, it would have to be my biology professor. Professor Smith looked at me as if I'd said a bad word during a church sermon as I quietly sat down. I mouthed "I'm sorry." He looked away and continued with his lecture on the anatomy of a frog. I blew out a heavy sigh and opened my notebook, trying to look as though I was hanging on his every word.

Chapter Fourteen

I made it to my business class after another painfully boring psychology class. I'm certain the class was dragging, because I was anxious to see Ryan. I could not concentrate on the topic of the Rorschach Inkblot Test, which was odd because it was similar to reading clouds. Instead, many things kept drifting through my mind. Would Ryan recognize me because I looked like Cathy and not Kat? And did he really like me or was he just being nice to me because Ryan was a nice guy? The thought of whether or not I should continue with the psychology class also crept into my mind, but it was too late to drop the class now. Too bad, I thought, as I drew clouds across the top of the page, making it look as though I was paying attention.

I probably walked faster to class than I needed to, since I was a little winded and flushed once I reached the door of the classroom. Yep, there was no way I could run a block at this point in my life. I stood to the side of the doorway, catching my breath, and scanned the room to see if Ryan was there. He was. And he was alone in the middle of the classroom. I guessed his buddies hadn't arrived yet. Do I dare push back the chicken known as Cathy, letting Kat step in and sit next to him? Butterflies were starting to flutter in my stomach, making me feel shaky and excited at the same time. What if he says no? What if he doesn't recognize me? No, he *had* to recognize me since he'd made that comment about being alone in the back of the classroom. That comment still stung when I thought about it.

Ryan was looking at his cell phone and didn't see me enter the room. I wondered if he was sending a text to a girlfriend. He was cute, so he had to have at least one girlfriend. I took a deep breath, gathering all the courage I had, and walked towards him. With each step, it felt as though I had to pull my foot out of the thick mud that seemed to be following me. I was thankful that Ryan did not hear me coming.

"Hi, Ryan," I said quietly, waiting for shock or annoyance.

He looked up from his phone. "Kat, it's you! I'm glad to see you again!" Relief bubbled inside of me as I got caught up in his smile. Yes, Ryan did seem very happy to see me. "Did you want to sit next to me, or were you going to sit in the back?" Ryan took the notebook that was in front of the empty seat and shoved it into his backpack. I guess I didn't have a choice. This time I ignored the "sitting in the back" comment. At least he didn't use the word "alone."

"That would be great, but what about your buddies?" I looked around to see if they had arrived and was happy to see that they hadn't.

"There are plenty of seats for them. Also, I spend more than enough time with them as it is. I was wondering if I was ever going to see you again. Did you find your girlfriend?" The sentences were flying out of his lips nonstop. It seemed that Ryan was a little nervous. I was shocked, because I thought I was the only one who got nervous.

"I did find her, back on the dance floor. I don't know how she does it. My feet were killing me by the time I stopped dancing with you." I smiled as I sat next to him. My smile was a combination of relief and happiness.

Ryan laughed as he moved his laptop closer to him. I looked at his laptop, thinking that I could ask Ryan about buying a laptop. I felt a little embarrassed pulling my notebook out of my backpack. I am so old-school, I thought. Both Ryan and I were getting ready to say something when the professor entered and quickly started today's lecture, causing us both to laugh. My shoulders sank as I picked up my pen and started writing, while Ryan started typing.

I was having a hard time focusing on the lecture. Every time I wrote in my notebook, I had to wonder what Ryan thought of me using a notebook and not a laptop. Images of being shunned in high school flashed into my head, but I pushed them back, thinking that this was *not* high school. It was also hard to focus since I was sitting next to Ryan. I would occasionally look at Ryan out of the corner of my eye. Sometimes I would catch him looking at me, which would make us both smile; other times I would see him focused on the screen of his laptop or what the professor was explaining. Warmth would surface each time I glanced in his direction. It wasn't the type of heat I felt when I got nervous. Instead, it reminded me of the warm feeling that flowed through my body whenever I drank peppermint tea. I smiled, enjoying the sensation, and turned my attention back to the professor.

Professor Gautier's voice became a drone in the distance as the tap, tap, tap of Ryan's fingers on the keyboard stirred my thoughts. It reminded me of Jane and the first time we met, when she was chasing after me to see if I was okay. I remembered the tap, tap, tap of her shoes against the concrete of the plaza. I remembered being scared. And now she was my new friend. It was amazing how in such a short time I started college, made a new friend, and now I was sitting next to a guy. Who would have guessed that Boring Cathy would have come this far? And then there was my writing. Just like Ryan's fingers moving across the keyboard, my hand now moved against the white paper. I felt calm whenever I let the words flow onto the page.

"Kat, Kat." Someone was whispering my name. I must have gotten lost in my thoughts and missed part of the lecture. I turned to see a concern look on Ryan's face. I looked into his eyes and smiled. Ryan's worried look disappeared and was replaced with a smile.

"Kat, are you okay?" Ryan asked, his hand resting on my shoulder.

I shook my head and noticed that everyone, including the professor, had left the classroom.

"I must have gotten lost in my thoughts – definitely not in the topic." I started to panic, thinking that I missed the assignment. "Ryan, did Professor Gautier give us an assignment?" There was distress in my voice and Ryan could tell.

"Nope, you're safe. There wasn't an assignment. I was worried about you. You got very still, almost as if you had fallen asleep in class. I'd take you out for a cup of coffee to tell you what you missed, but I have to run to my next class."

I felt guilty keeping Ryan after class like that. I knew what it was like to be late for a class, and I did not want that to happen to him. I put my notebook into my backpack and noticed that Ryan had already put the laptop into his backpack, zipped it up, and set it on the desk. I had to wonder how long I had been lost in my thoughts.

"I'm sorry for keeping you. I'm okay; I was just daydreaming. Maybe we can get coffee another time," I said, pushing myself up from the chair. Ryan also stood up, his tall frame towering over me. I had to wonder how tall he was. He had to have been at least six feet tall.

"Coffee raincheck it is, as long as you promise to tell me about your daydream," he said with a sly grin, looking down into my eyes. I never got tired of looking up to see his eyes. And then there was that smile. His smile melted away the panic that was taking hold of me.

We walked out of the classroom, with Ryan behind me, which made me a little nervous. At least I was wearing sneakers instead of spike heels this time. I was relieved that the mud had disappeared and seemed to have been replaced with clouds, because I felt like I was floating down the aisle and out the door.

"I have to run this way, but I'll talk to you later," Ryan said, as he turned to me and pointed his head in the opposite direction. I stood getting lost in his steel-blue eyes, unable to think or speak. Looking into his eyes was like looking into the vivid blue sky when not a single cloud could be seen for miles and miles, just an endless sea of blue. Ryan stood waiting, and staring down at me. I'm not certain if he was waiting for me to say something or if he wanted to say something himself. He still hadn't asked for my phone number, and I had to wonder why. I'd better say something now, or he would be late to class. I didn't want him to sit in the front row with the professor glaring at *him*.

"Yes, I'll talk to you later, Ryan." I turned and walked the other way, mentally slapping my hand on my forehead and thinking *"That* was all you could think to say to him?" I needed to walk in the same direction as Ryan, but it was safer to walk in the opposite direction. I could hear Ryan running, with each step making a soft thud on the wooden floor. I stopped. I wanted to look at him, even if he was running away from me. I turned and glanced over my shoulder to see the tall, dark, blurry figure that was Ryan at the other end of the hallway. He too had stopped. I could see his arm come up as he waved to me. The butterflies were once again madly fluttering in my chest as I waved back. I had to fight back an incredible urge to start skipping down the hallway, since I knew Ryan was still standing at the other end of the hallway, watching me.

Chapter Fifteen

I was waiting for Jane in our favorite corner of our favorite coffee shop. Every Thursday after classes, we got together to discuss our psychology class, which we both despised; the next assignment from Professor H; or Professor H himself. This time I had to tell Jane about sitting next to Ryan. I was as excited as a kid getting ready to share a secret as I squirmed in my cushioned chair, waiting for Jane to show up. I jumped every time the door opened, only to have to sit down and fidget some more. I was thinking I would have to get another mug of coffee if Jane did not show up soon.

After what felt like an hour of jumping out of my chair and hoping it was Jane, she finally rushed through the door. This time I did not jump. Jane ran over to the chair, reaching over to give me a brief hug, before plopping in her chair and almost knocking over the mug of coffee that was waiting for her. She was winded and her cheeks were flushed, as if she had just sprinted to the coffee shop in record time.

"Oh, Kat, I'm so sorry that I'm late. You would not believe Professor Thomason. She had to talk to me about one of my assignments. Can you believe that? Obviously it was not good enough for her. I don't think she likes me. I really think she has it in for me, and I don't understand why. What did I ever do to her?"

I had to laugh. I'm glad I'm not the only one with that problem.

"Anyway, how are you doing? How was your business class? I noticed that you basically ran out of class without saying goodbye after Professor Brown finished that boring topic of ink blots. I want you to know that I was crushed," Jane said, dropping her head towards her chest and making a pouty face. It was my turn to raise an eyebrow.

"Oh, Jane, you know you could never be crushed."

"That's not true – I *could* be crushed. Anyway, tell me what happened. Did you see Ryan?" Jane perked right up from her pretend sadness and moved to the edge of her seat, dying to know if I was a chicken or not.

"Welllll," I said very slowly, trying to make Jane wait for my good news.

"Yesssss?" She followed, just as slowly.

"I sat next to Ryan." I'm certain I was bouncing up and down in my chair as I shared my achievement. Jane clapped her hands as if she had just witnessed a spectacular circus act. My heart was singing. I'm not certain if it was because I had sat next to Ryan, or because of Jane's reaction.

"Oh, Kat, I am so happy to hear that, and I'm so very proud of you. I'm glad to hear that he recognized you. He did, right?"

"Yes, he did. In fact, he knew it was me right away and he was very excited to see me. I will tell you, Jane, I was very nervous about saying hi to him. I seriously thought I was going to chicken out. I'm glad I didn't! Anyway, enough about Ryan. We need to start thinking about our latest assignment for Professor H."

"Oh Kat, don't be such a downer. It's definitely more fun talking about Ryan than our latest assignment for Professor H." Jane sat back in her chair as if I had just told her that she was grounded from going out to play.

Ouch, I thought to myself. I never thought of myself as a downer. I guess I could be considered a downer at times. I decided to ignore the comment as I sat back in my chair, grabbing my mug of cold coffee. I should get another mug, since Jane and I might be here for a while.

"Did you want another cup of coffee? My treat, it's the least I can do," Jane asked, as she got up before I could answer. I swear, she could read my mind at times, I thought.

I placed the cold cup of coffee off to the side and sat back, enjoying the softness of the chair. I closed my eyes, letting the smell of coffee wafting through the little coffee shop soothe my nerves. So many emotions and thoughts were running through my mind – Jane's comment about my being a downer, sitting next to Ryan today, and Professor H. I also thought about the one question I had been meaning to ask Jane for some time.

"Oh Kat, where did you drift off to now?" Jane asked, in a somewhat sing-song voice.

I jerked up, with my eyes wide open, causing Jane to giggle as she placed a steaming mug of coffee in front of me. I'm glad I didn't cause her to spill any of it.

"Where were you just now?" Jane asked, as she returned to her chair.

I took a long whiff of the coffee, letting the aroma wake my senses before taking a sip. I was also taking my time since I was a little nervous. I wanted to ask Jane my question, but afraid of what she might say. I'm definitely not looking forward to another "Kat, don't be a downer" comment.

"Oh, I was just thinking about a few things." I took another drink, noticing that I had Jane on the edge of her seat. "Does Professor H make you nervous? I'm thinking the answer would be no, since you did ask him to dance. I was just thinking about it the other day when he once again asked me to stay after

111

class. He definitely makes *me* nervous." And once again I spewed the words out without taking a breath. Maybe I've had too much coffee, I thought.

Jane looked at me with her head tilted to one side, as she usually does whenever I go off on my speed-talking. "Are you done, Kat?" she asked with a smile. "Sometimes I do find him slightly intimidating, probably because he is a little older, but he *is* just like any other person."

I sat back, thinking about Professor H being like any other person. First Professor H being a person was hard to imagine. But Jane had a good point. Professor H really wasn't any more special than me, or Jane, or Ryan. That was an interesting way to look at Professor H, or really anyone. Sometimes Jane's outlook on life astounded me.

"Kat, I think we should change the subject, and I am really not in the mood to discuss any homework assignments. I think we should play a game," Jane said, with a somewhat wicked smile on her face. My stomach started to rumble in fear of what type of game Jane would like to play – spin the bottle; truth or dare.

"A game – what type of game were you thinking about, Jane?" I asked, my voice slightly wavering. I could feel the butterflies of fear start to stir. It was the same feeling I get whenever I'm around Professor H.

"Oh Kat, just relax. It will be fun – trust me. The game is to find out what your stripper name would be," Jane said, as if it were nothing.

"Stripper name," I repeated. I was confused. "Jane, what does that have to do with the assignment?"

"Nothing, really," she said. "I'm just trying to find out more about you, and sometimes you make it hard. I thought a game would help. Also, I have a theory."

I closed my book, reluctant to play along with Jane. "Okay, stripper name. Start," I said, leaning back to see what she was going to do next. If anything was silly, it was this game.

I could tell that Jane was happy that I agreed to her little game, since she had a sly smile. She reminded me of the Cheshire Cat in Alice in Wonderland.

"What was the name of your first animal?" she asked, as she leaned closer towards me from across the table. I felt as if I was being interviewed.

First animal, I thought? Now I was lost. I didn't remember having any animals growing up. Mom didn't have time for such nonsense. I looked off to the side, thinking about my first animal, hoping that I could pluck the memory out of the air.

"I remember finding a scrawny black cat that mom reluctantly agreed to let me keep. I'm almost certain I used some type of guilt trip to get her to let me keep the cat."

I sat back, trying to remember the name of that cat.

"I know the name of the cat started with a B." Again I had to pause as I tried to remember the name of that scrawny cat. I could see the black cat drinking water out of a bowl on our front porch. I also remembered the cat had bare patches of lost hair, probably from fighting with other alley cats.

"Now I remember. The cat's name was Barren. I know that seems like a strange name for a cat, but the poor thing had bare patches all over its little body." I sat upright, happy that I'd remembered the cat and its name. I was starting to like the game now.

"Barren," Jane repeated, sounding almost incredulous.

"Yes, Barren," I said. "I know it's an odd name. I'm not making it up".

"Kat, I believe you. But we're not done with the game."

Great, I thought, throwing myself back into the cushioned chair, feeling defeated and hating the game.

"Okay, now what was the first street you lived on as a child?" Jane asked, as the interviewing questions continued.

The first street I lived on – I said to myself – now that was easy. My mom and I lived in the same house for as long as I can remember, and that was on 47th Street.

"Forty-seventh Street," I said, not as enthusiastic as when I'd said Barren, because I was getting anxious wondering where Jane was going with her line of questioning.

"Oh Kat," Jane said, almost regretting that she'd asked to play this game. She sat back, still looking at me, but no longer with the Cheshire Cat smile. Instead she was biting her lower lip. This was not a good sign, I thought.

"It was worse than I thought," she whispered. "Your stripper name would be Barren 47th."

"Barren 47th, Barren 47th, Barren 47th" – I was repeating the name the way I had when I repeated the nickname Jane had given me. Only this time, sadness, not happiness, crept inside of me.

"I knew it," I said, "I knew it. Even my stripper name is boring. Jane, there's no hope for me. I am destined to be a boring and lonely person… just like my mom."

My hands quickly covered my mouth at the same instant that the words escaped. Damn, why was I always doing that?

"Kat, what did you just say?" Jane grabbed one of my hands, trying to move it from my mouth. "This is the first time I've heard you mention your mom. Is she still alive? I've always been afraid to ask, and you never mention her."

Now Jane was the one letting the words spew out without taking a breath.

"You always seemed to be alone," she added with a whisper.

Right now I wish we were at the pub, rather than the coffee shop, because I needed something stronger than cream in my coffee to share my story with Jane. Not that a light beer was that much stronger than cream. I moved my hands away from my mouth, letting them fall onto the table, and stared at them trying to find my story. In a sense I wanted to share my story with Jane, but I wasn't certain how – or how much. The anxious butterflies that had been rumbling in my stomach earlier were now at war. I took a long sip of my coffee, trying to find the strength, trying to find the words, trying to calm the butterflies that were beginning to feel more like bees.

"Come on, Cathy." Jane gently touched my shoulder, trying to reassure me. "You can tell me. Remember, I'm your friend."

I looked back up at Jane and then at my hands, thinking that Jane was right, she was my friend, but... But what? I let out a long, heavy sigh. I was lost.

"My mother is gone," I whispered. I sucked in a breath, trying to gather some more courage, and to push back the tears that were pooling in my eyes. "When she was around, all she would do was work, come home, and then go back to work. You see – boring, boring, boring. One day we had a fight, and I yelled at her, wishing she would go away, and she did. It's my fault that she's gone. Not only am I a bad person, I am a boring person." I could hear my voice getting louder with each word, because each word brought back painful memories. Each word brought back the fact that Mom was gone because of me.

I continued to look down at my hands as the words I'd just shared drifted through the silence. I had to wonder if Jane had heard me. Of course she'd heard me. I had to wonder if *everyone* in the coffee shop had heard me.

Jane did not say a word.

I looked up to see if Jane was still there, and she was. Jane was looking at me with sadness in her eyes and tears streaming down her face. She rushed over to me, grabbing me in a long, hard embrace.

"Oh, Cathy, I am so sorry to hear that your mom is gone. But it's not your fault and you are definitely not boring. It was just a silly game, and I'm so sorry for forcing you to play."

I stayed with the hug for as long as I could. I really thought she was going to cut off my oxygen – and maybe that would have been a good thing, I thought. I really do not deserve Jane's hugs or her kindness. While this hug was comforting at first, I now needed my space. I needed air. I needed to cry.

"Jane, it's okay." I pushed myself back, trying to get some distance between Jane and myself. Jane moved back to her chair, still looking at me with the same sad eyes that were now red and puffy from crying.

"Jane, you thought you had a feeling about something, and that was why you wanted to play the stupid game. What was it?" And then it came to me. Jane thought I was boring. I could feel the room getting hotter, or maybe it was just me. The buzzing in the pit of my stomach went from dread to utter disappointment. First I was a downer, and now I was boring. I swallowed the rage that was bubbling inside me.

"Jane, did you suspect that my name would be boring?" I asked. You really *do* think I'm boring."

Hearing those words was just as painful as feeling them, I thought. I was crushed. If Jane, my new friend, thought I was boring, then there was no hope for me. I might as well give up school and waste my life away at the pillow factory like my coworkers – just like Mom.

Just like Mom. The words vibrated in my mind. Just like Mom. I had to leave. I had to leave now before Jane saw me cry. I had to be alone.

"Jane, I'm sorry, but I have to go." I grabbed my bag and books, leaving Jane before she could say another miserable word to me. I stopped at the door of the coffee shop to take one more look at Jane, my so-called friend. She was standing next to our table with her shoulders slumped. Jane was staring at me in part disbelief, part sadness, and mouthed "Sorry." I turned my back to her and opened the door, rushing out of our favorite coffee shop.

Chapter Sixteen

It took longer than usual to get home. Perhaps it was because I was crying on the way home, and it was hard to see the road through my tears. Perhaps it was because I was distracted by repeating the last awful hour in my mind, and I made a few wrong turns. I was glad to be home, inside the walls that created my security bubble. I was also relieved that I did not have to work tonight. I would have called in sick if I did. I couldn't be around anyone right now. And really, who would want to be around Boring Cathy, the girl who caused her mom to disappear.

I looked at the ream of paper stacked on the small kitchen table. The urge to throw the paper across the kitchen was overwhelming. I ran over to the table, picking up the stack of paper, and froze. I heard a voice. The humming that had been constantly vibrating in my head had been replaced by a soothing voice. It was a woman's voice. Could it be Mom? Had she returned? I let the paper drop onto the table. Instead of falling into a neat stack, the paper fanned out, covering the table like a blanket of snow. Each piece of paper was calling out to me, patiently waiting for my attention. I sat down on the wooden chair, which groaned under my burden. My shoulders sagged and my head ached from crying.

I pulled a piece of paper from the blanket of white, pushing a few pages out of my way. The pages fluttered to the floor with a hush. The whiteness of the page was glaring back at me just like a mirror. I could still hear myself saying to Jane, "As boring as my mom" and "It's my fault." I closed my eyes, letting my head droop, with my chin almost touching my chest. I could see my mom swinging me around, just as she had in my dreams. I felt my heart drenching in guilt and breaking with loneliness. I saw myself drowning in the tears that I'd kept trapped inside me. I grabbed the pen and started writing. This time instead of writing "Who am I," I wrote "Dear Mom."

Dear Mom,

I don't know who you were, and now I never will. I do know that you cared for me and I know it was a challenge. I was not the easiest child to raise, and rarely was I the happiest child. I know I caused you heartache, and maybe I asked too much of your time. I know I did not show you the love that I should have, the love that I really did feel for you.

I wished you were here to tell me more about you. I wished you were here now so I can ask you questions about my childhood and your childhood. But because of me, and the awful words I said, I will never know. The guilt and the pain that I have been carrying since you left has swallowed me, leaving me to drift alone in the darkness. I keep praying that someday you will return, removing the blanket of darkness from my clutch and finally letting the sun and you touch me.

Mom, I always knew that you loved me, even though there were times when I felt you did not. It was so selfish of me to think that. I know you did the best you could.

Dearest Mother, I'm constantly wondering who I am – and at this point I know that I am your daughter. No matter how boring I may seem, or how plain, inside I know that I am and always will be your daughter. I hope that wherever you are, you can hear my words.

I wish I could take back the awful words I said the last time I saw you. I never wanted you to go away, but you did. I remember getting home early from school that day, excited to cook dinner for you. On my way home, I had found daffodils bursting with a yellow bloom in the alley behind our house. I picked two, one for each of us, and placed the flowers in a glass. I then set the flowers in the middle of the table. Dinner was ready, the table was set, and I waited and waited and waited. I sat alone in our tiny little dining room, watching daylight turn to night, with the darkness and the silence surrounding me.

Oh, Mom, why did you have to leave? I'm sorry for what I said. The guilt of those words haunts me every night when I go to bed, and every morning when I open my eyes.

Dearest Mother, I forgive you for those times when you tore my room apart. There were times when I heard you crying and did not try to comfort you. Please forgive me for not going to you when I heard you crying. You were as much alone as I was. It's so sad that we were two lost souls in the same house, and could never find each other.

Mom, please forgive me for the awful thing I said – and come back. I miss you.

I'm sorry I never told you that I love you, but I'm telling you now.

I love you and miss you, Mom.

Your daughter, Cathy

Tears were streaming down my face as I placed the pen on top of the paper. I was exhausted and my hand was aching. I placed my hot forehead on the table and sobbed until I could no longer cry. The tears had mingled with my words, causing some of the words to smear. I lifted my heavy head up from the table and pushed myself out of the chair. I wasn't certain how long I had been sitting and crying. It must have been a while, since my legs felt like lead. My feet tingled with each step I took as I dragged myself to the bathroom. I stood in front of the mirror, my image gazing back at me. I moved closer to the mirror, looking deeper into my puffy, blood-streaked eyes. I grabbed the counter of the bathroom sink and thought of my question, the question that had become a constant hum always whispering in the back of my mind. I took a deep breath, letting it out slowly, and stared into my hazel eyes.

"Who are you?" I asked, my voice raspy from crying.

I could hear the answer singing in the night as the wind gently blew through the trees, causing a branch to tap against the bathroom window. I am my mother's daughter, I thought. I could see Mom's eyes staring back at me. The eyes looking back at me were kind and overflowing with hope. I pushed myself away from the mirror and climbed into bed, wrapping myself in my blue comforter and relishing the warmth and comfort that it brought me.

The wind was whipping through my hair as I saw my feet getting closer and closer to the sky. Each time I swung back, I felt a gentle push on my back that propelled me forward and launched me even higher. I giggled as I saw my feet soar closer to the clouds each time. I imagined jumping out of the swing and onto the cloud. The puffy clouds were calling out for me, their song the breeze that whisked past my ears. Just a few more pushes and I should be able to touch the clouds. I looked back to see Mom, also giggling, as she pushed me towards my quest. Each time I swung back I would get a soothing breath of roses. I shouted "Higher and higher, Mommy!" Mom gave me one final push that sent me soaring into the heavens. I was like a bird with my arms outstretched, floating among the clouds. Little birds – some blue, some a soft brown – flew past me as they chirped a pretty song. Mist brushed across my cheeks and arms as I passed through one cloud and then another. I was weightless. I was free.

Chapter Seventeen

The light of a new day was peeking through the shades as I blinked my eyes, willing myself to wake up. I was exhausted. I tried to move my arms, only to find myself tangled in my blue comforter. I was wrapped like a cocoon. I moved to one side of the bed, trying to wiggle myself out, but I gave in to the battle, thinking that lying here was better than facing the day. I turned my head to my nightstand to see that I had about two hours before I had to be at work. I moaned, thinking about leaving my security bubble. It would be so nice to hide in my apartment all day, just the way I used to do. I guess I could hide in the fog of packing and taping boxes filled with pillows. The hum returned this time, it was a mental debate between whether I should hide or if I should be a big girl and go to work. It had been a while since I had seen Fred, and I was missing him and his jovial demeanor. I was certain Fred's smile would wash away some of my troubles.

Yes, Cathy, you need to put your big-girl panties on and get yourself out of bed, I thought. But for some reason, the voice in my head sounded a little deeper than mine.

I moaned, pulling one arm out of my comforter, and reached for my phone that I had left on the nightstand. Jane had called numerous times, starting from the time I ran out of the coffee shop to the last call about thirty minutes ago. I really needed to call her back, I thought, as I tossed the phone back on the nightstand and finished pulling my body from the blue cocoon. I swung my feet onto the floor and pushed myself off the bed. The cold floor felt good against my warm feet. The coldness made me feel alive. I shuffled to the bathroom, noticing that the letter I'd written to Mom last night was still on the kitchen table, just where I'd left it. I skipped the bathroom and walked over to the kitchen table. I looked down at the letter and noticed that a few of the words were smeared. There were also little splatters of black where my tears had fallen. "Dear Mom" had not been touched; neither were "I love you" and "I miss you." My heart started to throb, remembering last night.

I had to wonder, what if Jane had not wanted to play that silly game? I probably would still be stuck in the same Boring Cathy routine, always beating myself up for the past. I would continue to be oblivious about my feelings for my mom, feelings that I had buried so long ago. I really had to thank Jane, I thought. I walked over to the refrigerator with the letter, and placed the letter on the front of the refrigerator with the only two magnets I had. I let out a sigh, thinking that it had felt good to share some of my personal details with Jane. There was definitely more to share, but I wasn't certain I was ready for it. I lightly touched the letter with my fingertips, thinking that there were certain things that should remain between Mom and me.

I walked back to the bedroom and picked up my phone. I sat on the bed, propped myself up with two fluffy pillows, and dialed Jane's number. Her phone rang and rang and rang. She must still be asleep, I thought. I was getting ready to hang up when I heard, "Kat!"

"Kat, is that you?" Jane asked, slightly out of breath.

"Hey Jane, yes, it's me," I smiled. It was good to hear her voice.

"Are you okay? I was really worried about you since you left so quickly. I was afraid you would do something stupid, or that I would never hear from you again. I'm really sorry about the game. It was selfish on my part to force you to play that stupid game. Will you ever forgive me?"

I had to laugh, since I wondered if Jane was ever going to let me speak.

"Kat, Kat, are you still there?" Jane asked, gaining an octave towards the end.

"Yes, Jane, I'm here. I was just waiting until you were done," I said with a giggle.

Jane laughed, but it wasn't her usual gleeful laugh. I could tell she was relieved, but still nervous.

"Jane, it's okay," I said. "And yes, of course I forgive you. I really don't want to talk about it more than we already have, but it was good for me to tell you a little bit about me and my past. After I left, I went home and had a good cry. Now I feel better." I was surprised at how calm I sounded. I was wondering if someone else had taken over my body during the night, and I was looking down at her, just like a guardian angel.

"Did you want to get together today?" Jane asked.

"I have to work today, but I get off around 4:00. We can meet after I get off work. I was hoping that you could help me buy a laptop. I don't have one, and I decided that I really need one." My hand was still aching from last night.

"Also, Jane, we still have Professor H's latest assignment to do."

"Right," Jane said. I had to wonder if she stood at attention when she said that. "Again, Kat, I am really, really sorry about yesterday."

"I know, Jane, and everything is okay," I said – and I meant it. "Jane, I really need to get ready for work now. I'll call you later today to find out where we should meet."

"Sounds like a plan, Kat," Jane said, with her sweet and happy voice returning. Yes, everything was going to be okay, I thought.

I placed the phone back on the nightstand and looked at the clock. I still had an hour before work. I went back to the kitchen. Blank pages were scattered on the floor and across the table, bringing back the memory of last night. I bent down, picked up the few pages that were on the floor, and placed them on the table with the other pages. Once again the pages were calling out to me, a soft voice vibrating through my body. I sat and gazed at the paper thinking how pretty the page was, not touched or tainted in any way. It was pure. And when I placed words upon the sheet it would change. It would become more than what it was before. I picked up the pen, placing the tip to the blank page. The pen flew across the page with ease. Every word I wrote changed the page, with each page becoming different than the one before – the words from mind to hand to pen and then onto the paper, my words transforming the blank page into something different.

With the final stroke of the pen, I was at peace. Negative thoughts were banished as I transferred my deepest fears and feelings onto the paper. There were many things I could now do with this piece of paper, I thought. I could read the nonsense that I'd created. I could crush the paper into my hand, creating a paper ball that I could toss into the air. I could also throw the paper ball away, throwing my negative thoughts away. Or I could give it to Professor H to see if I am worthy to be in his class and prove him wrong.

After what I'd just gone through, anything transferred from my mind to paper should be tossed away and not read. I didn't have the energy to relive the past twenty-four hours again. I was spent.

The constant hum of "What if" played in the back of my mind. What if I wrote something that was really good, at least in the eyes of Professor H? No, I thought. I did not want to share this with Professor H, even if he thought it was a piece of art. I picked up the piece of paper and crushed it in my hand. I was in awe as I gazed at the paper ball in my hand, turning it in one direction and then another. I had transformed it from untouched to touched, from a piece of paper to a paper ball that allowed me to release what I had not been able to release in a long time.

On my way to the bathroom to shower, I threw the crumpled ball of paper into a trash can. I did not ask my question when I looked at myself in the mirror to brush my hair. The mist from the shower was still swirling in the small bathroom, causing my image to seem like a dream. I wiped my hand across the mirror to see my face looking back at me. A light was glittering around the outside of my hazel eyes. It was bouncing from me to the mirror and back again. I felt free. I smiled and enjoyed seeing my thin, pink lips smile back. Yes, I thought, I had a better sense of who I am.

Chapter Eighteen

I was happy to see Fred waiting in the breakroom when I got to work. I needed his sunny disposition right now. He looked up from his paper when he heard me enter the breakroom. A huge smile spread across his face, making his rosy cheeks plumper. I sat down after putting my coat in my locker to give Fred the usual update on classes and Jane. I hadn't seen him since the nightclub adventure, so I told him about Ryan. His smile got even bigger when I told him about Ryan, making me feel like a child again. Fred was such a funny guy, I thought to myself, but it was a good funny. A funny that always made me feel safe and cared for.

"So, kid, is everything okay? You seem a little different today."

Even though I *felt* different, I had to wonder what made me *seem* different. Were my eyes still puffy from crying most of the evening? No, I remembered looking at myself in the mirror before leaving for work, and my eyes were okay. In fact, they were more than just okay. But Fred had always been perceptive.

"No, Fred, I'm okay. Why do you ask?" I could tell my voice was a little shaky. Even though I felt safe around him, I knew I could not share with Fred what had happened last night between Jane and me, and what had happened afterwards.

"Oh, I don't know, kid" he said, moving closer towards me. "It's a little hard to explain, but you do seem a little more at ease. Since I've known you, you've always seemed melancholy just like your mom. I know that working at the pillow factory could make even the happiest person gloomy. But now you don't seem so blue."

I sat rigid, feeling my walls coming back. "Just like Mom" played over and over in my mind. I knew that Fred had worked with Mom, but I'd never had the courage to ask him what had happened to her. I didn't want to hear the words that had become my truth. And then I thought, "What if?"

"Fred, am I really like Mom?" I asked, very slowly, since I wasn't certain how Fred would react to the question. He moved around in his chair, uncomfortable by the question. He coughed into his hand, clearing his throat.

"Cathy. Your mom was a very sweet woman. She was a hard worker, probably one of the hardest I ever knew. I think you get that from her." Fred paused, shifting his gaze from me to the side of the breakroom. A distant look replaced the happy demeanor in his bluish-gray eyes. Was he looking for the next words to say, or was he thinking of Mom? I wondered if Fred had waited at the table for Mom when she started her shift. I smiled, thinking that he had. Fred took a deep breath before continuing.

"Your mom had a hard life raising you by herself. Just the way I do with you, I would ask her how she was doing before she started her shift. Like you, she was my ray of sunshine in this dismal place," he said, sweeping one arm off to the side.

I smiled when I heard that Fred also watched over Mom. But why, I thought – and ray of sunshine? Fred was probably the nicest guy I knew, but I never saw him waiting to talk to any of the other female workers. Fred and Mom seemed close, apparently closer than I knew. I sat back in the metal chair waiting for Fred to share more about Mom, but instead the silence returned. Rarely was there silence between Fred and me. However, the silence was not heavy or awkward – instead, it was comforting. We were both lost in our own thoughts, our own memories. Fred coughed into his hand again, pulling me back to the breakroom. The table shifted as Fred moved forward in his chair. He placed his hands on top of mine. I could feel the warmth and love from his touch.

"Cathy, I loved your mom very much. She was a very special person to me, and so are you," Fred said, his voice slightly quivering with emotion.

I blinked back the tears that were threatening. I looked up at Fred and noticed that his bluish-gray eyes were glistening. I swallowed. Why hadn't I seen it before? Fred's eyes were a reflection of mine. And then everything fell into place. I pulled one of my hands out from under Fred's and placed it on top of his. I gently squeezed his hand and smiled.

"I love you, Fred." I pulled my hands away from his and pushed myself up from the chair and over to Fred, giving him a big hug. I wrapped both arms around him and I placed my tear-stained cheek onto his left shoulder. I could feel Fred's chest sinking from the huge sigh of relief he had just released. He returned the hug, stroking the back of my head just the way a parent or grandparent would do when comforting their child.

"Okay, kid, time to get to work," Fred said, in a soft and gentle voice.

I swallowed the realization and the feelings that were caught in my throat before letting go of Fred.

I did not have to worry about losing myself in the haze of filling and packing one box after another with pillows, and then moving the boxes from one side of the huge warehouse to the other. No, my thoughts were tied to Mom, Fred, and my girlfriend Jane. Once again I had the feeling that I was someone else, and that the real Cathy was floating above me. Between the constant hum, and the effortlessness of my body and mind moving through the warehouse, I lost track of time. I probably would have worked past the end of my shift if Fred had not tapped me on the shoulder with a tender chuckle.

"Okay kid, time to go home. Do you have a date with Ryan or Jane?" Fred asked.

"I do have a date with Jane. She's going to help me buy a laptop," I gleefully responded.

"Now that sounds like fun. You'd better get going. You don't want to keep Jane waiting," Fred said, laughing.

I had to laugh since Jane doesn't wait for anyone. It's usually the other way around.

Chapter Nineteen

I jumped into my car and drove to the nearest Best Buy. I was surprised to see that Jane was patiently waiting for me as I pulled into a parking spot just in front of the store. Wow, she *was* waiting for me, I thought.

Jane skipped towards me once she saw me get out of the car. I chose to jog instead of skipping, since I knew I would definitely trip if I tried to skip. Even though I was happy to see Jane, I could not join her in her happy dance of jumping up and down once we were face to face. Instead, I gave her a hug.

"Oh Kat, I am so happy that you asked me to join you. I have the perfect laptop in mind for you," Jane said, as she grabbed my hand and pulled me towards the double doors of the store.

The doors automatically swung open as we walked up to the huge store. I had to blink a few times to adjust my eyes to the bright lights. I was overwhelmed. I looked to my left and then my right, wondering where to start. I was so pleased with myself for thinking of asking for Jane's help that I gave myself a mental pat on the back.

"Now Kat, while I do know a few things about laptops and have something in mind for you, I think we'd better find someone from the Geek Squad."

The Geek Squad, I thought. What the heck was a Geek Squad? It seemed like code to me, but then again, I was looking at laptops.

Jane was now holding onto my sleeve and tugging me over to a counter, as if I was her rag doll. Above the counter was a sign that said "Geek Squad." To the left of the counter was an endless display of laptops in various sizes and colors. My mouth dropped and my stomach churned when I looked at the never ending rows of laptops.

Jane saw a tall guy wearing a blue shirt with his back to us. It looked like the guy was fixing or playing with one of the laptops. Jane walked up to the tall guy, authority oozing from every pore, and tapped him on the shoulder. I decided it would be safer if I stayed at the counter below the "Geek Squad" sign and just watched.

"Excuse me, but I was hoping that you could help us. My girlfriend needs a laptop." The tall guy in the blue shirt turned to face Jane.

I didn't know what dropped more, my stomach or my mouth. I'm glad that neither Jane nor Ryan could see my mouth hanging open. Yes, it was Ryan, the Ryan from the nightclub, and the Ryan from my business class. I had just gotten off work, and I probably *looked* as though I had just gotten off work with my hair in its usual unruliness. I needed to find a bathroom, I thought. I looked to my right and then to my left, but it was not obvious where the bathrooms were. Wait a second, I thought, I'm concerned about how I look. This has got to be a first. I shrugged my shoulders and decided to take a chance.

Jane was walking towards me, with Ryan following close behind. "Ryan, this is my friend...."

"Kat?" Ryan asked, in a mixture of disbelief and excitement. At least it seemed like excitement to me. Maybe I was fantasizing.

"You know Kat? Wait a second, you're *that* Ryan?" Jane said, looking at me with both of her eyebrows moving up and down several times as if she'd just trapped me.

"Yes, Jane, this is the Ryan I told you about," I said, trying to fight back the nerves. What was Ryan going to think about my telling Jane about him?

"I see," Jane said, crossing her arms in front of her chest and tapping her foot.

"Seriously, Jane, how was I to know that Ryan worked here? And besides, you were the one who picked this store." I felt as though I was on trial, with Jane and her authoritative stance.

Ryan just stood several feet back, waiting for Jane and me to finish our little banter. I had to wonder what was going on in his mind, especially when both Jane and I referred to him as "*that* Ryan." Now he knows that I've talked about him. I wondered if that was a good thing or a bad thing. He did have a huge grin on his face, so I had to think it was a good thing.

"Okay, Jane, now that you have brought Ryan over here to help, we should probably make the most of it," I said, trying to change the topic.

Jane and I both turned to Ryan, who stopped grinning as best he could and went into work mode. Ryan started to asked question after question about what I was looking for in a laptop. Yes, Geek Squad *does* equal speaking in code. I was getting confused and overwhelmed with all the questions. I finally had to stop his litany of questions.

"Ryan," I interrupted him by gently placing my hand on his shoulder, as the heat from his body quickly radiated into my hand.

"I really do not know a thing about laptops or computers. I need something that I can use for my classes, like our business class and my writing class. What would you recommend?" I had to wonder if that was a dangerous question, since he could recommend the most expensive one. Right now, I was thinking I really didn't care. I was also thinking how wonderfully odd it was to bump into Ryan.

And there came the smile. He was beaming. I'm not certain if he was smiling because I still had my hand on his shoulder, or because I was putting him in charge of deciding which computer I should get.

"Okay, Kat, I know exactly what you need. Trust me," Ryan said, with the sly smile returning.

Thirty minutes and several hundred dollars later, I had the perfect computer – blue with a matching case. Ryan got all the operating systems and software installed. He tested the laptop to make sure everything was working properly. I blushed as he handed me the blue bag that carried my new laptop, and his card. I finally had his number, I thought. Yes, I was floating just like one of those puffy clouds I loved to watch. I was floating as if in a dream.

Chapter Twenty

I got home, still riding on cloud nine. I flipped on the kitchen light before plopping myself, along with my new blue computer bag, onto the couch. A blissful groan drifted through my body. It felt so good to sink my body into the soft cushions of my couch, I thought. I closed my eyes, enjoying the softness that surrounded me. A flash of a smiling Ryan replaced the blackness behind my eyes, bringing on a big smile. I wrapped my arms around myself, savoring the pure joy that was pulsating through my body. I could get used to this feeling, I thought.

I opened my eyes to see the light reflecting off the paper that was still scattered across the kitchen table. I was admiring the unique halo hovering over the kitchen table. Yes, the paper was calling out to me. Even though I had a childlike urge to play with my new laptop, the need to write on paper was overwhelming. One more night, I thought.

I pushed myself from the comforts of the couch and moved to the kitchen. I grabbed my favorite red mug from the cabinet and made a cup of steaming peppermint tea. I breathed in the minty fragrance, letting the steam kiss my nose. With mug in hand and the sweet aroma circling my head, I walked over to the CD player. Instead of Maroon 5, I decided to listen to Beethoven's Moonlight Sonata. Professor H suggested that we should listen to the sonata when writing since the music would relax us. I sat back in the wooden chair, tilting my head back slightly. I continued my blissful float as the music played softly in the background. I closed my eyes, letting the soft sound of the piano sweep my light body away. But soon, sadness crept into my heart and branched out to my limbs with each keystroke. The distinct notes moved into my fingertips as the notes got higher and higher, and then dropped. My heart also dropped – but then it burst open. Rays of light shattered my darkness, and through those rays I saw the face of Mom. She was smiling at me – something I had rarely seen. Her love was surrounding me like a warm embrace. She had always been with me, but I had lost her in my confusion and guilt. I took a deep breath, unleashing years of tears and sorrow. I felt Mom hugging me as I wrapped my arms tighter around myself, taking in all of her essences.

Memories drifted in and out of my mind. I plucked out those memories and placed them on the paper. The whiteness of the paper was quickly replaced with feelings that I had forgotten, or did not fully understand. I wrote about a love that was always there, but never fully realized. I wrote about a love that left too soon, and a love that I should have recognized but was too blinded to see through my selfishness. I wrote about the dreams I had for moving forward. Page after page was filled with words that I had pushed to the darkest depths of my mind; each word forming line after line until the page was no longer white. When I thought I had nothing left, I pushed out the last line of suppressed thoughts and feelings.

I sat back in the chair, looking at the paper that was no longer white but shades of black, thinking, "Who am I?" There was just enough space at the end of the page to write a few more words. I stared at the small space and in a faint voice asked, "Who am I"? With a mind of its own, my hand quickly glided across the bottom of the page, writing "I am whoever I want to be."

I placed the pen down, my hands shaking. I lifted myself out of the chair and walked to my bathroom mirror. I stared in the mirror looking at my reflection, just as I had so many times before. My eyes did not seem as lifeless as they had been a few days, weeks, months, or even a year ago. They seemed more alive, with a tiny light sparkling at the edge of my iris, almost as if they were twinkling at me. The dark shroud that I had been wearing as a shield for so long had been replaced with a faint aura pulsating around my body.

I took a deep breath, my eyes still locked on the person who was gazing back at me. "Who are you?" I softly said in a steady voice. The light above the mirror flickered. I jumped and looked up to the light. The light flickered again. This time I did not jump. Instead, I just stared at the light. Was that the answer to my question – "I can be whoever I want to be," I thought?

I always knew I had a guardian angel watching over me. I now had to wonder if Mom was that angel, and she was reaching out to me. I moved my hand to my heart, swirling in this realization. Was that where she went? She somehow made it to heaven to secretly watch over me?

"Oh Mom, I really should have said I loved you instead of what I did say. Please forgive me for saying those awful things to you," I said in a raspy voice. "I really did love you, and I'm sad that I never had a chance to tell you that." I let out a heavy sigh, letting my forehead rest on the cold mirror.

"Mom, I hope you knew that I loved you," I said, my voice cracking with regret.

The light flickered several more times. And then it was dark. My heart dropped. The only sound I could hear was the sound of my breath, in and out, in and out, as I tried to calm myself. Yes, Mom was letting me know that she understood. I took that thought and wrapped it around myself, just as my mom had wrapped her arms around me when I was five.

I steadied myself, my hands holding onto the bathroom sink, willing myself to move out of the darkness and back into the kitchen. I could tell that each breath fogged the mirror as the gentle mist hit my cheeks. A cracking sound pierced the darkness and silence that engulfed me. I didn't have to open my eyes to know what had happened. I didn't need a light to know that my mirror had just cracked. Laughter erupted from my body. I should really be crying, I thought. The one thing that I had relied on every morning for the last year decided it was no longer needed.

The laughter and the cracking sound both stopped, as the humming that had become another constant in my life returned. At first I hated the sound. It reminded me of flies buzzing around my head in the summertime. Now I looked forward to it. It felt like someone, maybe Mom, was singing to me. This time, however, jumbled words floated in and out with the hum. I closed my eyes, forcing my mind to focus on the words, the voice – a soothing voice calling my name – but there was more than just my name. And then the voice and the humming were gone. My eyes flew open and a wave of dizziness surged through me. I wrapped my fingers tighter around the edge of the sink to support myself while my eyes adjusted and the wooziness passed.

The light from the kitchen filtered into the bathroom, bringing a glimmer into the darkness. A flashback of my previous nightmares came back, but not the anxious terror. There was no need for me to be afraid anymore. I turned away from the cracked mirror and fumbled my way out of the bathroom and into the kitchen. My heart was pounding. I placed one hand on my chest in an effort to keep my heart from beating out of my chest. I eased myself onto the couch, sinking deep into its soft cushions. I took several deep breaths, extending the exhale a little longer each time, hoping my heartbeat would return to normal. The hum had returned, but now as a whisper that was barely noticeable. I was able to hear the fluttering of my heart and my own voice talking to me. I now had a better understanding of Mom and me. There was one more mystery left to unravel.

Chapter Twenty-one

The sky was gray as I walked across campus to my favorite bench. The brisk wind whipped my hair in front of my face. I was mentally kicking myself for leaving the apartment without a hat. I pulled the collar of my jacket closer around my neck, hoping to keep out some of the cold. I should really buy a scarf, I thought, as I came upon the bench. I looked at the trio of barren trees that guarded my bench. The smaller branches quivered in the wind as if they too were fighting against the cold that surrounded us. I sat down on the wooden bench and gazed at the sea of gray churning above me, unable to read a single cloud. The sky was one huge cloud that hovered above me. I closed my eyes and sat back onto the bench, feeling the cold wind brush against my cheek. I took a deep breath, feeling a hint of moisture enter my body. Visions of Ryan came to mind, bringing a smile to my face. Even the thought of Ryan's smile brought warmth to my cold body.

The sound of the wind whistling through trees lulled me to my dream world. I could see myself floating in the sea of gray. An incredible urge to stretch my arms out, as if I was getting ready to soar through the sky, bubbled to the surface. A scuffing sound on the concrete squashed that impulse. Scuffing sound. Who else would be on campus, especially on a miserable day like today, I thought? I opened my eyes to see a faint shadow on the ground, looming in front of me. Fear immediately pushed down all the happiness I had been feeling and brought me back to the ground. I slowly turned to my right to see Professor Hanson staring down at me.

My heart jumped as anxiety stirred in my chest and my breathing became erratic. I will never be at ease with this guy, I thought.

"Funny, I thought I was the only one who knew about this bench," Professor H said, as the hint of a smile broke through the stony face that I'd grown accustomed to in the classroom. I did notice that he was the smart one as I saw the ends of his blue scarf, dancing around his neck.

"I was surprised when I got your call, asking to meet you at this spot. Do you mind if I sit next to you?" Professor H asked, with what I could only detect as some warmth behind his words. Where was the warmth coming from, I had to wonder? The fact that I called him? Or that we were not in his classroom, his sanctuary?

Professor H waited for me to give him the okay. He waited, looking down at me, his hands stuffed in the pockets of his leather jacket. I looked down to the ground, noticing that he was wearing jeans and running shoes instead of his usual khakis and brown shoes. Wow, he almost seemed normal, I thought. Flashbacks of the first day of class returned. He was just as close now as he had been then. I could smell a hint of citrus and pine drifting with the wind. I wished he had been wearing that scent the first day of class, since it brought back happy memories of exploring the woods when I was little. Maybe then I could have written something more than just two cryptic lines.

I could tell he was fidgeting, as his shadow swayed in front of me. Just like the dark clouds above us, his request was hanging heavy in the air. I'd better say something, and soon. I could just see him taking off without another word, and then what? Would he take it out on me in the next assignment? And to think that I'd been the one who'd called him. Why did I call him? For once I had an impulse, and I followed through with it. I was mentally kicking myself, and frantically trying to understand why I wanted to talk to him. I swallowed, trying to get my dry throat to work. I knew I needed to say something, and I needed to say it soon. I did not want to come off like an idiot again.

"Hmm, sure." Was that it, I thought? Was that the only thing I could think of? I moved slightly over to the left of the bench, giving Professor H some room. A gust of wind hit me, causing a few strands of my hair to fly across my face. I brushed the strands behind my ear, again cursing myself for not wearing a hat.

I kept my eyes fixated on a small rock that had somehow found its way onto the concrete plaza. I didn't want to look at him – not with him sitting next to me. My self-doubt started to creep back in, taking over whatever confidence I'd gained over the past week. Professor H would never see me as anything other than one of his boring students, I thought. I guess it's still hard for me to let go of the Boring Cathy stigma. It's a coat that I've been wearing for such a long time.

I could feel the small space between us vibrate. Maybe the vibration was my own shaking, because of the cold and dread seeping into the core of my body, or maybe it was because stony Professor H was sitting next to me. I'm not certain what was affecting me more, the silence between us or the anxiety that was taking over my body. Once again, words escaped me, and my mental chant of what to say buzzed in my mind. I thought maybe if I had a piece of paper I could write down what I was feeling or what I wanted to say. But then again, I tend to panic whenever Professor H hands me a blank piece of paper.

"Cathy, are you going to tell me why you called, or will I have to guess?" he said with a huff, interrupting my mental discussion and breaking the silence like an ice pick chipping at a block of ice. Each word out of his mouth was just as frigid as the wind blowing through my hair.

Ouch! I guess he *hasn't* changed. His earlier warmth and smile were just a façade, I thought. He will always be the ever-so-icy and abrasive Professor Hanson that I've grown to know. I don't know what I was thinking when I dialed his number. It was that damn voice I heard last night. The voice was whispering, "Cathy, Cathy, are you there?" I knew it was a man's voice, but the voice was also soothing – so why would I have thought it could have been Professor H? Clearly I was not thinking straight after all that had happened last night.

"I, I need to know why you are so mean to me in class," I said softly, stuttering the words out and hoping that maybe he would not hear me.

A heavy sigh escaped from Professor H. Was it annoyance or relief? I couldn't tell, and it made me feel even more uncomfortable than I already was. The bench moaned as Professor H leaned back.

"Oh, Cathy, I'm not mean to you. I guess you could say I've been a little hard on you, especially in the beginning. I knew you were better than those two cryptic lines you wrote the first day of class. I didn't want you to be like the other girls who were taking the class just to stare at me and follow my every more. You're better than that. I knew you could be more than just a girl who sits and watches. I knew you were the girl who could listen to me. I wanted you to listen to me and to learn from me." His voice was going in and out like a dream as

I grasped onto the meaning of each word he spoke. Once again, it felt as if I were suspended in space watching, almost as though I was a bird perched on a branch, gazing down on Professor H and me.

He coughed into his hand before continuing. For some strange reason the cough eased my tension, instead of heightening it. I didn't jump and move away from him – I just sat, frozen in time, hanging on to his every word.

"I know that most of the girls in my class signed up for it just because of my looks, and not because of me or the subject matter. I was simply a statue for them to admire. I kept hoping that someday I would find a student I could transform, a student I could inspire." His body turned slightly in my direction and looked at me. "Cathy, I think you are that student," Professor H said, this time with warmth and hope behind his words.

I was afraid to move, but not because I was sitting next to Professor H. I was afraid that if I moved I would discover that I was dreaming. Could Professor H really believe I had potential – me, Boring Cathy? Was he challenging me to be better than what I thought I was? I mulled this over and over in my mind, liking the way it felt. And then I remembered what Jane had said about someone coming into your life at just the right time. You do not understand it at the time, but it just feels right. I had to laugh to myself, because Professor H didn't feel right – or even comfortable. He was quite the opposite. He was hard and cold, almost like the bench we were both sitting on. I took a chance to glance over to Professor H to see him looking up into the heavens; his jaw was relaxed making his face appear tranquil.

My body instantly relaxed. I felt as though I was finally floating in the sea of gray that was looking down at us. All the tension, anxiety, and self-doubt that I had been carrying for so long melted away. The wall I had erected was being chipped to pieces.

"Do you really think I have potential?" I said softly, the words wavering from the realization that someone could think that of me.

"Yes, Cathy, I do, and I want you to realize that potential. It's not enough for me to see it. You are the one who has to see it. You are the one who has to believe it," Professor H said, with something I had never heard before in his voice. There was passion in his voice. The statue that I had created was beginning to melt.

Once again I felt his gaze, but this time it did not feel like the cold laser I'd endured the first day of class. It was warm, almost inviting. It was similar to the feeling I get when Fred looks up from his paper as I enter the breakroom, or when Mom was watching me sing "Silent Night." It was a look of admiration. The frigid wind that had been whipping around us was gone. Instead the air was still, and not as cold. Professor H cleared his throat before pushing himself off the bench. He stood in front of me, casting his shadow over me.

"Cathy, why don't you let me walk you to your car?" he said, extending his hand for me to grab.

I moved my attention to his hand, admiring his long fingers and noticing that they were a bright pink. I guess he wasn't as smart as I thought he was, since he was not wearing gloves. I placed my gloved fingers into his palm, proud of myself for wearing gloves. Even though his fingers were pink, I could feel the heat from his hand through my gloves. He pulled me up, making me stand in front of him and forcing me to look into his dark eyes. His eyes were not as dark and gloomy as they were before. Instead, his eyes reminded me of coffee after I've added just a touch of milk. He moved to the side, still holding my hand, and started to walk. I followed in silence as he guided me across the plaza and to the parking lot.

We stopped at my car, and he released my hand. I dug into my purse for the car keys and unlocked the door. His arm slowly reached for the door handle and opened the door. I turned to face him and to whisper "good bye," since I didn't know what else to say. I was drowning in an emotional haze, with confusion and happiness swirling around me, making it hard to think. Even though I was not afraid to look into his eyes, I decided to keep my focus on the dimple in the middle of his chin. His hands came up towards me, brushing a strand of hair behind my ear and then pulling the collar of my jacket closer together.

"You should get home and warm up," he said, his voice still filled with kindness. I looked up to see that he was looking at me, and our eyes locked. There was no fear boiling in my stomach; there were no cold fingers of dread wrapping themselves around me. There was just the hum. I closed my eyes, wishing that I could say more to him, such as "thank you" or "have a nice day," but I could not. There was nothing more I wanted to say. Instead, I turned and slid my body into the car. The car door shut with a thud. I blinked open my eyes, released a heavy sigh, and started the car. I backed out of the parking spot and drove away to see Professor H standing as still as a statue in my rear-view mirror. He did not wave. He did not smile. He just watched.

Chapter Twenty-two

I strolled across the campus, reminiscing about my first semester as a college student. I could not believe it was already coming to an end. Once again I'd let time slip through my hands – but this time it was good. I wasn't sitting idle in my apartment. I was living, and at times I was floating. It seemed like only yesterday I was walking across the campus to my first class, watching one foot step in front of the other, with my eyes focused on the ground. Now I glanced from one side to the other, observing all that surrounded me. The weather was brisk, with a few snowflakes swirling down from the gray skies. I wrapped my new blue scarf a little tighter around my neck, and thrust my hands deeper into my pocket.

The plaza was not as busy as it usually was. It must be because of the weather, because who in their right mind would sit or stand out in this weather, I thought? I picked up my pace, trying to outwalk the wind, when I heard "Kat, Kat!" It didn't sound like Jane. I stopped and turned to see a smiling Ryan jogging towards me. Instead of my breath catching in my throat, my heart fluttered and I instantly smiled.

"Kat, wait for me," Ryan called out as he continued jogging towards me.

I would be gasping between words if I were jogging, I thought. Even with the snow flurries whipping around me, I felt warm as Ryan's smile got bigger and he got closer. He stopped, not even breathless, and gave me a hug. I wrapped my arms around him and squeezed, enjoying the warmth of his body and the smell of Ivory soap.

"What are you doing here? I didn't think you had a final today," I said, enjoying his arms around me. It reminded me of the feeling I get whenever I am wrapped in my blue comforter.

"I just wanted to wish you good luck on your writing final. Are you nervous?" Ryan asked, releasing his comforting hug and shoving his hands into his pockets. I was grateful that he stood close to me, creating a wall between me and the wind and snow flurries.

Nervous, I thought – if he only knew. Even after my conversation with Professor H, the thought of having to write in his class brought back the anxious dread I'd felt the first day of class. I seemed to write better outside of class, I thought, without Professor H looming in the background.

"Hey Kat, are you okay? There's nothing to be nervous about. I know you'll do great," Ryan said, placing his strong hand lightly on my shoulder. Just like Jane, I thought. I believed that Ryan could read my mind. Ryan's hand on my shoulder was the support that I needed.

I looked up into his steel-blue eyes, seeing a caring and concerned person staring back at me. Ryan was right. I can do this. I can do anything, I thought.

"Ryan, you are the best," I said, staying lost in the eyes and the comfort that was Ryan. "You're right. I have nothing to be nervous about."

"Well, don't be nervous. I'll be at the coffee shop if you'd like to get coffee after your final?"

"Jane and I will be there after our finals. We were going to talk about the final assignment and then start studying for psychology."

I could see a hint of disappointment on Ryan's adorable face, which seemed out of place. I felt bad. I hated disappointing Ryan. It was my turn to place a hand on his shoulder, which was more challenging for me since Ryan was at least a foot taller than me.

"But you can definitely join us," I quickly added.

The smile returned, and Ryan wrapped both arms around me, allowing my overextended arm to go from his shoulder to around his waist. I placed my head on his chest, enjoying the fluttering of butterflies in my body and the pounding of his heart.

"You bet. I'll see if I can't save us a table," Ryan said, squeezing me a little tighter.

"Ryan, I'd better go. Finals will be starting soon, and I do not want to be late."

I really didn't want to let go. I closed my eyes and took a deep breath of Ivory soap and the essences of Ryan. Ryan released his grip, bringing his hands to my shoulders and moving me slightly away from him. I automatically looked up to get another glimpse into his eyes. Ryan was bending down, bringing his face closer to me. The butterflies that had been humming throughout our embrace were now fluttering like crazy. I was afraid that if I opened my mouth, the butterflies would escape. Was he going to kiss me, I thought? I closed my eyes, part anticipation and part alarm. My heart was racing. And then I felt his lips softly touch mine. I melted. The kiss was warm and tender, reminding me of the mist that surrounded me after a shower.

Now I really didn't want to let go, I thought. I did not want to turn and walk into the building that was behind me. I wanted to stay in this moment for as long as I could. Ryan slowly pulled his lips away from mine. I sighed, but it was a good sigh.

"Hey Kat, are you okay" Ryan whispered. I could hear the uncertainty in his voice. Why should he be afraid, I thought?

"Yes, I am *very* okay," I said, as I looked up and smiled. Now it was Ryan's turn to smile back. I had to wonder if my smile was as infectious to him as his was to me. "It may be a little hard for me to concentrate now."

The sly grin that I remembered seeing when Jane and I bumped into Ryan at Best Buy returned. I think he was no longer uncertain or afraid, but pretty proud of himself.

"Okay, now I have to go," I said, amazed that my lips were able to move after his kiss.

I slid my hand down to touch his hand, our fingers intertwined. I did not want to let go of his hand, but I knew that if I didn't move now, I would be late for class. I turned and slowly walked away, letting my fingers hold onto his for as long as they could. I was floating on a cloud. Ryan released my grasp and ran ahead of me to open the door. I gave him one last smile before walking through the doors and down the hallway to my first final. I thought about skipping, but not with everyone else running to their finals. I had to wonder if Ryan was still watching me. I stopped and glanced over my shoulder to see that he was. I waved and resumed my walk. I will let my heart do the skipping for me, I smiled.

Chapter Twenty-three

I was relieved when I got to my creative writing class to see that I was not late. In fact, there were only a few students in the classroom. I decided to stick with my usual seat in the back of the classroom. I realized that I enjoyed sitting in the back, not to hide but to watch. I was always entertained by the girls who strolled into class. Sometimes I would admire them, and sometimes I would giggle to myself because of the outfits they'd decided to wear that day.

As usual, Jane walked in a minute before class was to start, looking polished as always. Her hair did seem to be styled differently. I had to wonder if she was going to make her move after she turned in her final, and was prepping herself for the kill. I waved at her as she took her usual seat, in the center of the third row. It was the perfect spot for Professor H to see her and for Jane to keep an eye on Professor H. Jane waved back, with a huge grin on her face, before gracefully sitting down. Yep, she was up to something, I thought. I had to admire her.

The class was bustling, probably with anticipation for Professor Hanson to stroll into the room. I knew he had arrived even before the class did, even before the silence indicated his arrival. He walked into the classroom and over to the board with his usual saunter. In the past, he would scan the room before walking over to the board, but not this time. He seemed more distant than usual as he wrote our final assignment on the board. As I had feared, it was the assignment we'd had the first day of class – the Assignment from Hell. Yet, instead of just one or two sentences, Professor H wanted us to write at least a page about ourselves and our experience of being in his class.

Even though my confidence had improved, flashbacks of that horrible first day returned, causing my breathing to feel out of control. I knew I was able to write about myself now, but that was in the comfort of my tiny apartment. I was also uncertain what I wanted to write about regarding my experience in his classroom. Should I dare be honest about the intimidation and the mixed emotions I experienced every time I stepped into the classroom, and every time I got ready to leave? And why would he care about our experience? Maybe he wants to know if he has had an impact on any of us. I looked up from my desk, understanding the reason behind his second request. And there he was, Professor H, sitting at the edge of his desk and looking out into the classroom – but more toward the back of the classroom. Yes, he was looking at me. Our eyes met just the way they had yesterday, and he gave me a slight nod. Yes, I can do this, I thought.

Professor H pushed himself off the desk, grabbing the stack of paper. Just as on the first day of class, he went to each row, giving the first person a small stack of paper. It seemed as though it was taking him longer to reach me than it had that first day. I took a few deep breaths, trying to calm my nerves, as I watched him move closer and closer to me. Only two more rows, and then, there he was standing next to me.

"Cathy," he said, as he handed the last of the stack to me. I was relieved to hear that his voice wasn't as cold as I thought it would be. In fact, it was almost a soothing whisper. I looked up to see that his face was not the usually rigid mask that he wears when in the classroom. The jawline had softened, just the way it had yesterday. I reached for the paper wondering if I was flushing, since my cheeks felt extremely hot.

"Thank you, Professor Hanson," I whispered, moving my gaze to my desk and waiting for him to turn away before handing the stack down my row.

"Do you have a pen?" Professor H added with a sly grin. I glanced up to see Professor H looking down at me with a twinkle in his coffee-brown eyes.

"That's pretty funny, Professor Hanson," I said, with an equally clever grin, lifting my hand off the desk to show him the two pens I had. The sly grin turned into a full smile before he turned away from me.

I pushed myself off my chair and handed the small stack of paper to the guy who was several desks away. I could hear each soft step Professor H made as he walked down the aisle and back to his desk.

I sat back in my chair, giving all my attention to the blank piece of paper that was reflecting back to me. I gently skimmed my hand across the page, enjoying the feel of the paper. I looked back to the board to read the assignment once more. "Your experience in the class," I said to myself. The tension was starting to rumble even more, turning into a wave of panic. I thought about the class ending, and that brought sadness to my heart. I started to look forward to the ritual of Professor H asking to see me after class. Once the class ends, so does the ritual, I thought. I could not tell him that I believed he was too young and too good looking to be a professor. I could not tell him that he intimidated me. I took a deep breath, letting it out slowly and hoping that the long exhale would clear my mind and pull my swirling thoughts into something tangible and meaningful. I looked at the pen that was still in my hand. I looked at the blank piece of paper staring back at me. This time, I did not feel as though the starkness of the paper was taunting me. It was inviting me to spill my feelings onto it. Ryan was right. I can do this, I thought. I took another deep breath and placed the tip of the pen onto the paper, letting my words flow onto the page.

Throughout my first semester as a college student, I gradually discovered many things. I discovered how to be a friend and how to be a student. I discovered that I can choose to be a shadow hiding in the background, or I can be like a bird, soaring above everyone. At one time, I feared this blank page because it would stare back at me, mocking me, and also because I did not know who I was. I came to realize that this blank piece of paper was the door to an endless world of possibilities. I can write about the daughter that I should have been. I can write about the type of mother I thought I wanted. I can write about the hardships that any mother-and-daughter relationship may face and eventually endure. I can be a person filled with excitement, or I can choose to be someone boring who walks in the shadows trying to get by. I can make sense of a world that seemed to be a mystery to me. I can love myself, because I am a good person. I can be the best friend I was meant to be. I can be a person with dreams that are floating in the clouds, waiting to be snatched and written down. I can even be a girlfriend to a tall, good-looking guy. I can turn my bees of anxiety into butterflies of hope. I can learn to forgive myself and accept the fact that I am good.

My experience in this class has revealed to me that I can transform this blank page into something that is more than it was in the beginning. This page is my domain. The words in my head spinning around are meant to be seen so that they can inspire. This blank piece of paper is my canvas to explore the "What ifs" of my life. What if I did not choose to go to college? What if I decided to just stay in my tiny apartment? What if I did not open my heart for friendship or love? My "What ifs" transform potential regrets into hope. My "What ifs" transformed me into someone who answered the question that I have been asking myself for too long. "Who am I," you asked. Here is my answer: I am whoever I want to be.

I put the pen down. I am finally at peace. No more struggling. No more feeling of dread. No more beating myself up for the awful things I said to Mom. I am free.

I calmly pushed myself out of my chair, grabbing the page and walking down the aisle towards Professor H. My legs felt light, almost as if I were walking on a cloud. The mud was gone and so was the humming. Just as on the first day of class, Professor H was focused on the stack of papers that had already been turned in. I knew Jane's final was there, and I had to wonder if she had written her phone number on the paper. I wasn't concerned with trying to be quiet, as I had been on the first day in class. In fact, I was determined to smile at Professor H when he looked up at me. My heart and breathing were steady. The only sounds were those of pen on paper and my steps crunching on the carpet. Neither sound was disturbing Professor H. He remained as still as a statue, his focus on the paper in front of him. I quietly placed my paper on the desk, thinking that he would look up and grab the paper, but he did not. I stood next to the side of the desk, the spot that I knew so well and despised so much. And still he did not look at me. I shrugged my shoulders, turning to the doors, and slowly walked away, half expecting him to call out my name the way he had so many times before. Instead of my name I heard the crunch, crunch, crunch of my feet padding across the carpet. I pushed open the door, feeling a breeze brush against my cheek and the dark hallway pulsating into view. I looked down one end of the hallway and then the other, trying to find Jane. She was not waiting for me. The only thing I saw was a glimmer of light at the end of the hallway.

Chapter Twenty-four

Maybe Jane decided to wait for me at the coffee shop, I thought, deciding to walk in that direction. I pushed open the door, hearing the familiar squeak of the old hinges. I was surprised to see that the coffee shop was almost empty. The place was strangely quiet for a morning as the wooden floor creaked with each step I took. I scanned the coffee shop and noticed one person sitting alone, engrossed in a book, oblivious to the creaking. There was another couple sitting on the other side, who looked up from their cozy huddle as I passed by. I gave them a brief smile and continued my trek to my favorite corner. I was disappointed to see that Jane was not sitting in her usual chair. I was hoping she'd have a mug of coffee waiting for me. Maybe she was still waiting for the coffee, I thought.

I came around the corner to my favorite spot, and froze. There was Ryan, casually sitting in my chair, in my favorite corner. I stopped dead in my tracks, wondering how he could have known. Ryan did not hear me, since he was looking out the window, lost in his own thoughts. I stood as still as I could, watching him, and wondering if he could feel my gaze. He did, as he slowly turned his head in my direction, and smiled. I smiled back, feeling the warmth from his smile move to the center of my chest. He stood up from the small cushioned chair and walked over to me, grabbing my hand. An overwhelming feeling of comfort washed over me.

"How did you know this was my favorite spot?" I asked softly. I was a little confused that he would be sitting at my table and that Jane was not with him. I looked from one side of the shop to the other, waiting for Jane to walk towards us carrying our coffee.

"Ryan, where is Jane?" I asked, with an edge of concern in my voice.

"Shh, Kat, it's going to be okay. Why don't you sit down," Ryan said, pulling out a chair for me to sit in, but he was not pulling out my usual chair. He was pulling out the chair that Jane usually sat in. I was confused. And why would he "shh" me, I thought? The look on his face was calming and assertive at the same time. I reluctantly turned to sit down when I noticed something on the chair. I bent down to get a closer look. It was a single red rose. I took a small gasp, shocked by what I saw. I picked up the rose, bringing the beautiful blossom to my nose. I closed my eyes and took a deep breath, letting the sweet scent flood my senses. Tears surfaced, as thoughts of Mom came rushing to my mind.

"Kat, are you okay? I hope the rose wasn't too much. I just wanted you to know how much I care for you. The instant I saw you I knew there was a connection between us," Ryan said. The calm and assertive voice that I'd heard earlier was now wavering. The nervous Ryan was back.

I blinked back the tears that were threatening to pour from my eyes. Oh Mom, I love you, I thought. I turned and threw my arms around Ryan, almost knocking the tall guy over. I gave him the hug that I had been dying to give him since that night at the nightclub.

Ryan laughed, wrapping his arms around me and lifting my feet slightly off the wooden floor.

"Ryan, it's perfect. I love roses."

Ryan slowly lowered me to the floor, releasing his grip and bringing his hands up to my shoulders. I looked up, excited, when I saw him leaning closer to me, thinking that I was going to get another kiss. Instead, Ryan lightly pressed his lips to my forehead. The heat from his lips was an inviting sensation that radiated from my forehead to every inch of my body. Even after he pulled his lips away, I could still feel the heat on my forehead. I turned, placing my cheek on his chest, to hear the thump, thump, thump of his heart. I smiled. And to think I thought that only happened to me.

I blinked back the tears to see that the light above us was flickering.

Chapter Twenty-five

The light was blinding. I turned to my side to see that the sun was just starting to rise, with an orange haze floating around me. The words were already in my mouth before I'd had time to blink the sleep out of my eyes. I knew today would be the day. I could just feel it. The dread that I had carried for so long had been replaced with strength and optimism. The voices that had been a jumbled garble, and at other times a constant hum, were getting louder, pulling me out of the fog. I quietly slid my body out of the warmth of my blue comforter and floated across the floor.

I looked down to see that the tile had been replaced with the same orange haze. My feet disappeared with each step. With a childlike glee, I watched the fog part with each step, sometimes walking to the right and then the left, just to see what would happen.

The question was eager to be spoken – "Who am I, who am I." It was my own battle hymn, but I knew I was no longer going off to war. I was ready to break free of the guilt and the loneliness I had wrapped around myself. I laughed, thinking that the guilt and loneliness was my security blanket. Not anymore, I thought. Today will be my day.

I followed the foggy path that was taking me to the mirror. The morning light was just breaking through the small window in the bathroom, its rose and lavender haze reflecting off the mirror. I stood with the words humming on the edge of my tongue. I grabbed onto the porcelain sink just as I had so many times before. Like the tile floor it was cold, but I did not shiver. My eyes were already staring back at me, almost as if my reflection had been waiting for me, waiting for this day. My eyes were telling me that it was time.

I leaned forward, bringing myself closer to the reflection. I smiled, hoping that the thin, pink lips would crack a smile, and they did. Though my brown hair was in disarray, it added to the person that was staring back at me. Yes, my life at times seemed to be in disarray, but it was *my* life, and I was okay with that. I focused back on my eyes and asked the question. The three little words, "Who am I?" eased from my lips. The hesitation and fear were gone. Instead there was acceptance.

"Cathy, Cathy, can you hear me? Are you awake?" A deep and soothing voice emerged out of the fog.

Warm, strong hands touched my shoulders, lightly rocking them. The heat from the hands moved into my body, causing my heart to flutter. I turned to the voice and tried to open my eyes, but couldn't. My eyelids were heavy. I felt heavy. I was feeling light just a moment ago. Why am I feeling so heavy now?

"Cathy, Cathy..." There was that voice again, this time with a hint of urgency behind my name. I willed my eyes to open so that I could see who was calling me. Wait, he called me Cathy, not Kat, I thought. I'm Kat. And why was this person in my bedroom?

I heard the soft tap, tap, tap coming towards me. Could that be Jane, I thought? Jane was the only one who tapped like that, but this tap was softer, almost more like a shuffle. I turned to the sound to see slits of light breaking through the darkness. A shadowy figure leaned over me. The hint of flowers after a gentle rain washed over me. I could feel the edges of my mouth slightly curl up. There was a halo around the face that was floating above me. At first I thought it was my guardian angel gazing down at me. I blinked again to see that the woman had a mixture of concern and relief on her pretty porcelain face.

"Jane?" I whispered, her name barely escaping my lips. I licked my lips, feeling that they were as dry as my throat.

"You gave us a scare. Now just take it easy. You've been out for several days. The doctor will be happy to see that you're finally awake. How do you feel?" Jane's soft and soothing voice was almost enough to lull me back to sleep, but I resisted. Instead I blinked my eyes several times, forcing them to stay open, but the light was so blinding. Fluorescent lights were glaring down on me, almost burning my skin. I closed my eyes, turning my head to the side and away from the glare.

"Why didn't you wait for me?" I whispered, still trying to find my voice.

"Now, now, Cathy, just take it easy. I think you've been dreaming," Jane said, gently patting my shoulders.

"Jane, why are you calling me Cathy? You are the one who gave me the nickname Kat. And why do you keep telling me to take it easy? Is there something wrong with me?" I asked. The fear that I thought I had conquered was bubbling back and erasing the fluttering from the warm touch. Why was Jane calling me Cathy? And why am I lying down? Did I faint after Ryan gave me the rose? Thoughts of Ryan, his smile, and the rose flooded back, pushing down the fear that was fighting to return. I squeezed my eyes shut to keep the vision of Ryan locked in my mind.

"Cathy, try to keep your eyes open. I will dim the lights so they are not so bright."

I heard a quick shuffle across the tile, fading away from me, the click of a switch, and then the shuffle returning. There was a soft, swooshing sound as Jane sat down on a chair that was next to me.

"Okay, Cathy, slowly open your eyes," Jane said softly.

I gradually opened my eyes. My eyelids were not as heavy. The brightness of the room was no longer blinding, but instead had a warm, orange glow. I turned towards Jane and smiled. I was so happy to see her, but she looked different. She was not wearing her pretty white summer dress or leather leggings. She was dressed in a simple, dark-pink smock. The gold chains and hoops were missing, replaced now with a badge hanging around her neck. The badge had a picture of a smiling Jane.

"Jane, where am I?" I asked.

"You're in the hospital. You have been here for almost a week. I was beginning to wonder if you decided you were going to be like Sleeping Beauty and never wake up," Jane said, with a touch of humor.

"Hospital! Did I faint?" I asked, alarm in my voice. I pushed my body up from the bed, resting on my forearms.

"The doctor wasn't quite sure what happened to you. From your reaction, I guess you don't remember," Jane said, the concern in her voice returning. "I'm going to go get the doctor. But first, I need to introduce you to your new friend."

Jane looked over to the other side of the bed. My head followed to see the source of the strong hand and deep voice.

"Ryan, it's you. Did I faint after you gave me the rose?" I asked, as excitement and relief replaced the fear that was overtaking my body. The feelings were temporary when I saw him look to Jane with both eyebrows raised.

"Ryan, is something wrong?" Now I was panicking. Why was he looking at Jane that way? It was always Jane and Professor H that would raise their eyebrows at me, never Ryan.

"I don't remember giving you a rose, but I can quickly change that," Ryan said, returning his attention to me and grinning.

I automatically smiled back, sinking down into the bed with relief and happiness. Wait a second, why was Ryan here?

"Ryan, I'm happy to see you but why are you here?" I asked.

"Cathy, Ryan is the paramedic who brought you to the hospital," Jane said. "He's been by your side every day," Jane said, bending down to get closer to the side of my face. I could feel her breath tickling my ear. "I think he likes you," she whispered. I could hear the smile behind her words, and my heart started fluttering again.

"Hey, I heard that," Ryan said with a chuckle.

I scooted myself up on the bed to get a better look at Ryan, when I froze. A presence that I knew all too well had just entered the room. I didn't have to hear the footsteps to know that he was here. I just felt it. Jane sensed it too, since she turned in the direction of the door. She nodded before standing and moving to the side of the bed. I swallowed hard, afraid of what he would say. Even the dim lighting was reflecting off his wire-framed glasses, shooting darts of light in my direction. And there he was – the Doc. The ever-so-cute and intimidating Doctor Hanson, the man who came into my life soon after Mom left. I fell back, praying that I could sink deeper into the bed and disappear. I knew he was going to reprimand me for not getting in contact with him sooner. This was not the ideal setting for getting back together after I missed our last appointment. I watched him gracefully stroll across the floor, sitting down in the chair with the cool arrogance that always put me on edge. He moved the chair, bringing his dark-brown eyes closer to me. I sucked in what breath I could, preparing myself for the lecture.

"Cathy, it is good to see that you finally woke up. You had several of us worried, with a number of unanswered questions," Doctor Hanson said, with a very slight edge of relief in his stern voice. He folded his hands in his lap and observed me. His chiseled features were not as rigid as I remembered. I blinked several times to clear a blurry vision that was floating in my mind. This was not the icy-cold Professor Hanson. This was the professor who walked me to my car, the one who was concerned for me. And then the vision cleared, and I understood. The memory hit me like a cold slap in the face. I remembered seeing myself in the bathroom. The steam and the citrus scent were gone. Just the darkness, the cold floor, and the pills scattered across the floor remained. Did I take the pills? I don't remember. Oh think, Cathy, think! I wanted to smack my forehead with my palm, but not with Ryan sitting next to me. You didn't do something stupid, did you, I thought?

I turned to Doctor Hanson, afraid to ask my question. "Doc, did I take the pills?" I asked, my voice wavering, afraid to know the answer.

Doctor Hanson bent over, pushing a strand of hair behind my ear. "No, Cathy, you did not. I was afraid that you had, but I couldn't find any traces of the drug in your body. I'm not certain what happened. Were you aware that your bathroom mirror was cracked?" Doctor Hanson said.

I wasn't certain which brought the tears to the surface, the concern in his voice or the fear that I could have allowed my depression to take over my body. And my mirror was cracked? How did that happen?

"How did you find me?" I asked.

"I got worried when you ran out of our last appointment. I knew you were upset, and being upset can lead to bad things. I called Fred to see if he had a key or if he could check on you. He didn't have a key, so the only option we had was to call 911. He and Ryan found you in your bed, wrapped in your comforter. I arrived shortly after the police opened your door. You were breathing, so that was a good sign, but the pills on the bathroom floor and the cracked mirror were not. Ryan rushed you to the hospital and has been here with you ever since," Doctor Hanson said, looking at Ryan with a nod of approval – and from what I could tell, gratitude.

The casual tone in his voice was familiar and somewhat comforting. I closed my eyes, lying as still as I could and processing every word Doctor Hanson said. I racked my brain, trying to remember our last appointment. What would have upset me and caused me to leave the appointment early? I knew I didn't enjoy our weekly meetings, but I was learning to endure them. Think, Cathy, think. What could have happened? I dug deep in my mind, playing out the scenes of the past week over and over, and trying to separate what was a dream from what was real. Was there really a distinction, I wondered? I swiped through each memory – coffee with Jane, the stack of white paper, Professor H saying I had potential, Ryan's smile, and then the lost little girl. When I thought I couldn't dig any deeper, a memory from the depths of my mind bubbled to the surface. I saw the mirror shatter and the light flicker, and then I remembered. I remembered what happened to Mom. A sigh escaped my lips and tears leaked from my eyes. I felt the soft touch of a finger sweeping away the tears from my cheek.

Time had stopped, and once again silence surrounded me. However, this silence was not hanging heavy like the dark cloud I had been carrying. This silence was one of understanding and compassion. I knew everyone in this room cared from me. And that included Mom, who was looking down on me. Mom was in heaven now. Not because of those awful words that spewed out of my mouth when I snapped. She was in heaven because of the car accident that took her away from me. I rolled to my side, my body no longer heavy. I curled my body into a fetal position, imagining my blue comforter wrapped snugly around me. And I cried. I cried, releasing all the sorrow, guilt, and tears that had been with me over the last year, my sobbing washing away the silence. A warm hand gently rubbed my back. I didn't know if it was Jane, Ryan, or Doctor Hanson, and that was okay. What I did know was that the person comforting me cared for me, and that was better than my blue comforter.

Chapter Twenty-six

My body was exhausted by the time the last tear fell. I opened my eyes to see that Jane, Ryan, and Doctor Hanson were still surrounding me, patiently waiting for me to return. I pushed myself out of the fetal position and sat up. Jane instantly placed another pillow behind me so that I could comfortably sit up.

"Ryan, do you mind if I have a moment with Cathy?" Doctor Hanson asked, with combination of authority and tenderness, something that only he could pull off.

"Not a problem, Doctor," Ryan said, his eyes locked on me when he spoke, rather than looking at Doctor Hanson. He bent towards me, bringing his lips close to my ear. I took a big gulp, still recovering from my onslaught of tears, to get a whiff of Ryan, thinking, "Nice, Cathy, right in front of him." The scent wasn't quite Ivory soap, but it was fresh, with a hint of pine. I closed my eyes, thinking of the forest after a storm, and wondering what he was going to do or say. This time it was Ryan who whispered in my ear. "I'll make a deal with you. If you are still here when I return, I will call you Kat. To tell you the truth, the name suits you," he said with a smile.

A playful smile broke across my tear-stricken face.

"It's a deal," I whispered back, turning my head towards Ryan and taking another deep but silent breath.

I watched Ryan walk out of the room, wondering if he would stop and glance over his shoulders just the way he had in my dream, but then I stopped. "It was just a dream, Cathy," I said to myself. Ryan had walked past Jane and Doctor Hanson, grabbing onto the frame of the door. And then he hesitated. My heart stopped. Ryan turned and glanced over his shoulder. Our eyes met, and we both smiled. Just like my dream, I thought. What did someone once tell me? Someone coming into your life just at the right time and you don't understand why – you just know that it feels right. Yes, that would have to be Ryan, I thought.

Doctor Hanson cleared his throat, unfortunately pulling me out of my dream and back to the dim hospital room. I blinked a few times before turning my head to him. I was not looking forward to this conversation. A flashback of sitting in a huge, soft chair in a bright office filled with leather furniture, bookcases, and a large desk settled in my mind. It was *his* office, the office that had become my second home where I tried to talk about Mom, my feelings, my insecurities, and my guilt. I was legally an adult by the time Mom passed away, but the social worker was concerned for my welfare – and rightly so. I was distraught. And that was when Doctor Hanson entered my life.

Once a week he would try to pull something out of me. In the beginning, our meetings were heavy with silence. He would ask a question and wait. The only sound between his questions was that of the clock ticking away the time until I was released. It wasn't until he had given me a journal that I started to break out of that silence.

It had been a long time since I had received a present. It was wrapped in pink-and-blue paper, with a huge pink bow that flowed across it. I looked up at Doctor Hanson when he handed the pretty package to me. My shaky hand took the package, wondering who had wrapped it – definitely not the

Doc, I thought. I slowly unwrapped the present, feeling as if I was five and it was Christmas morning. Behind the pretty paper was a beautiful, light-blue journal with colorful butterflies scattered across the front and back covers. Strands of gold swirled around the butterflies. I carefully opened the book to see blank page after blank page. There was only one page that had any writing, and that was the first page. It was an inscription in Doctor Hanson's handwriting, right in the center of the page:

"Forgiveness is a gift that you give yourself."

I closed the book, looking up at Doctor Hanson, and let the tears stream down my cheeks. He sat there just the way he had a few moments ago and waited, patiently waited just as he had for months and months, waited for me to open up. That was a month ago. I hadn't had the courage to write in the journal. I did flip through the blank pages and wondered what I possibly could write. While I did not spill what dark thoughts were packed tightly in my head, I did start to open up to Doctor Hanson, letting my voice replace the silence.

The last time Doctor Hanson and I met, I started to chip away at my guilt and finally began to understand the words that Doctor Hanson had been trying to tell me for almost a year. It was not my fault; it was not my fault – I remembered him saying that to me. The pain and realization hit me hard, like a wave crashing down on me. After so many days and months of believing in an illusion, the truth was too shocking to grasp, so I bolted out of his office and ran to my apartment. The only thing I remember was being incredibly sad, lost, and lonely.

"Cathy," Doctor Hanson said softly. "Do you remember what happened?"

Doctor Hanson must have seen the memories churning in my head, or maybe he can read my mind. I looked into his eyes, seeing their warmth instead of the cold darkness that was my reality for so long.

"Yes," I whispered. "Yes, Doc, I remember." I felt I should cry, but I was spent. I had no more tears left to cry. Perhaps I didn't need to cry anymore, because now I understood.

"Did you want to talk about it?" he asked, gently placing his hand on mine and reassuring me that it would be okay. My head was throbbing, perhaps from crying, or maybe because of all the painful memories I had just pulled from my darkness.

"No, not right now, Doc. I'm not certain what happened when I got home after rushing out of your office. Right now, it is all still so blurry. Maybe I hit my head or something," I said, moving my gaze back to the white blanket that covered my legs.

"Maybe…" Doctor Hanson added, but I sensed he was not buying it.

It was time to change the topic, I thought. "Do you remember the journal you gave me?" I asked, my voice oddly steady and normal, almost as if I felt in control.

"Yes, of course, Cathy," Doctor Hanson said. "I noticed it on your nightstand when we went into your apartment. I also noticed that you hadn't written in it yet." Even though he had toned down the disappointment in his voice, I could still feel it, but I chose to ignore it.

"Did you happen to bring it?" I asked, feeling hopeful that just maybe he had. The urge to write was overwhelming. The tips of my fingers were pulsating with the need to write my recent dream and my revelations onto those blank pages. Doctor Hanson turned to the metal nightstand that was off to the side of my bed.

"Yes. Here you go, Cathy. I'm wondering if I should wrap it again," Doctor Hanson said with the hint of a smile as he handing me the journal.

It was nice to see him smile, I thought. Not as nice as Ryan, but it was still nice. It was definitely a lot better than the placid face I used to stare at when he was waiting for me to talk.

"I'm going to let you get some rest. I think you should be able to go home tomorrow or the next day. We will talk some more in the morning. I'm also going to let Fred know you are awake. He too was very concerned about you, and spent a great deal of time sitting next to the bed watching over you. I'm certain he will want to see you tomorrow," Doctor Hanson said, pushing himself out of the chair.

"You mean Fred from work?" I asked excitedly. If anyone was the stable and happy part of my life, it was Fred. My tired and cry-ridden body came alive when I thought of seeing Fred and his wonderful, jovial smile.

"Yes, Fred from work," Doctor Hanson said with a grin, happy to see my excitement.

"Tell Fred I cannot wait to see him," I said, feeling as excited as a child getting ready to leave on an adventure and wondering if Jane or Doctor Hanson could see me bouncing on the bed, because that was how I felt.

Doctor Hanson's smile continued to grow as he turned his back to me and headed to the door. I watched as he walked away from me, wondering if he could feel my gaze. He did not flinch; he did not stop; he just strolled out of the room.

"Cathy, you should drink something," Jane said, handing me a blue cup with a long straw and pulling my attention to her. I had forgotten that Jane was still in the room. I smiled and obediently took the cup, bringing the straw to my parched lips, and took a long drink. The cool water felt good going down my dry throat. I could feel the water seep into every cell of my body, making me feel refreshed.

"I will be back in a bit to check on you."

"Jane?" I said as Jane was placing the blue cup back on top the beige metal nightstand. Jane stopped and sat back in the chair where Doctor Hanson had been sitting.

"What's up, Cathy? Are you feeling okay?" Jane asked, tilting her head to one side and placing her hand softly on my shoulder. Instead of feeling heat from her touch, I felt compassion and devotion. I had to think that like Ryan and Fred, Jane had also stayed with me night after night while I tried to dream my life away.

"Can I get a hug?" I whispered, still somewhat afraid, since really I had just met Jane.

A huge smile spread across her pretty, porcelain face. Without saying another word, Jane bent over, circling both arms around me. I reached up and wrapped both arms around her, feeling her heart beat and my body relax.

Chapter Twenty-seven

Jane and Doctor Hanson had left. I was alone, something that I was familiar and comfortable with, but this time it felt strange. It wasn't because I was sitting in a hospital bed, tethered to a monitored that flashed and hummed. It wasn't because I was without my blue comforter. It was because of me. I was different. Could a simple dream have put my troubled mind at ease, I thought? But it wasn't just a simple dream; it was more than that. I remembered Mom, and I remember telling her that I loved her. I remembered the flickering light, her signal to me that she understood. I remembered the mirror, which held my reflection, cracking. I remembered the paper that would taunt me, but most importantly I remembered asking that stupid question – "Who am I?" – and finally discovering the answer. A dream helped me find the answers – and the resolution I had been struggling with for the last year.

I propped myself up on the bed, bending my legs to my chest. I wrapped my arms around my legs and rested my head on my knees. The only sound in the room was the hum of the monitors vibrating through the room. I thought of Mom pushing me in the swing. I thought of her arms wrapped around me as she swung me in a circle. The humming reminded me of a lullaby that I had long forgotten, another memory that I had pushed into the depths of my mind. I remembered that Mom would half sing and half hum to me every night when she tucked me into bed. She would gently stroke my head, smoothing out my long, brown hair.

"Oh Mom, I miss you," I whispered into my hospital gown.

A knock, knock broke through my memory, preventing me from returning to my self-induced state of misery. I looked up to see Ryan standing in the doorway. He wasn't smiling. He was just standing, his gaze on me with a worried look on his face. Was he afraid to enter, especially after seeing me bawl like a baby, I thought?

"I'm glad to see that you didn't bolt from your hospital room," Ryan said, with a slight grin on his face. I let out a happy sigh and smiled.

"Well, you did promise to call me Kat if I stayed," I said, sitting up a little taller on the bed but keeping my legs bent and my arms wrapped around them.

"Do you mind if I come back into your room?" Ryan asked, still standing in the doorway as if some type of force field was preventing him for entering.

"I definitely cannot let my favorite nurse leave without thanking him. I hope it's okay to call you nurse?" I said, a little surprised at being so forward. A huge smile erupted on he's face, letting me know that either he liked being called a nurse or he liked the fact that I was being bold.

"Only if you also include 'favorite' when you call me nurse," he responded, seating himself in the same chair that Doctor Hanson and Jane had used.

My heart sank to see that Ryan and the chair were not closer. "What to say, what to say" played in my mind. I really didn't know this Ryan. Could this Ryan be the same caring and happy Ryan that I dreamt about?

"How are you feeling, Kat?" Ryan asked pulling me back to him.

And there it *was,* the smile that I had grown to love taking over his face. Yep, the tall, cute guy sitting next to me was the same Ryan I dreamt about.

"I'm doing better, but I'm tired of staying in this bed," I said, unfolding my legs and strategically moving the cover to the side. I swung my legs off the bed so that I was facing Ryan. Ryan looked into my eyes, causing my breath to catch in my throat and my heart to jump several beats. And just as in my dream, I got lost in a sea of blue.

"Ryan, I wanted to thank you for saving my life and for staying here at the hospital while I slept," I said, with what I hoped was tenderness. Ryan brought his hand up to my face, brushed a strand of hair behind my ear and beamed.

"Kat, I know this may sound very strange, but the first time I saw you I knew that I had to be with you. Call me crazy, but I had to stay with you until you woke up to see if I was right. Perhaps it was the paramedic in me, being overly concerned with a patient, but I really think it goes beyond that," he said, and then dropped his gaze down to the floor. Maybe he was afraid that I would bolt now, or coil in fear, but his words felt right. For once in a very long time, *everything* felt right.

I reached over and placed a hand on his knee. Ryan looked up, his face relaxed in a loving smile.

"I have something for you, but you have to promise me something," he added, as he lifted his other arm up towards me. I looked down to see a rose, a single red rose. My tears were returning but these were tears of happiness. Even so, I blinked the tears back since Ryan had seen more than enough tears from me, and I didn't want *him* to be the one who bolted.

"Oh, Ryan, it's beautiful," I said, reaching out for the flower. He snatched the flower away as if we were playing a game.

"Not so fast! You still have to promise me that you won't faint," he said, with a sly grin.

"I promise!" I said, as I jumped off the bed and into Ryan's arms. He circled his strong arms around me and swung me around and around. I was feeling light once again, just as though I was flying through the sky. Yes, I thought, I was finally free!

I couldn't tell, since I was being twirled in a circle, but I swear the light was flickering. Yes, I thought, Mom was letting me know that she was still watching over me, and that she was happy because I was finally at peace.